Two Sisters

The Dynamic Duo, Pilgrimage To Eternity

RACHEL ESTHER LEWIS

Kind, Loving, Generous, And Resilient Women Who
Selflessly Loved Their Families And Who Were Beyond
Reproach In This Life, Thus Inspiring Role Models
For This Generation And All Future Generations, All
Without Expected, Deserved, And Due Reciprocity
From Their Family Members During Their Benevolent
Inhabitance On This Planet And Pilgrimage To Eternity.

By Rachel Esther Lewis

TABLE OF CONTENTS

CHAPTER ONE

Young Sisters In Claremont, New Hampshire, Whose Parents Suffered Through "The Great Depression" And It's Sequelae, Which Forever Influenced And Shaped The Lives And Perspectives Of These Dynamic Duo Sisters. Navigating Elementary School And High School In The Post-Depression Era.

Sharon was married to a cattle ranch owner in Iowa. She had a young daughter, Jane, who was approximately six years old, with her husband and was hoping to realize the amazing married life with her husband that she had always envisioned and dreamed of as a young daughter of her parents. However, Sharon's husband was a serial spouse abuser, to the shock and dismay of Sharon, which was becoming more and more frequent after the birth of their only child, Jane, their beloved six-year-old gift from God. In the 1920's, Protestant Christian women who were subject to physical abuse by their spouses had few options to deal with this dilemma. Divorce is forbidden in the Bible and was, thus, not recommended or advised by Sharon's church leaders, unless the couple failed marital counseling, an extremely perilous situation was apparent, or unless, for other reasons, divorce was absolutely essential.

Sharon, after years of enduring physical abuse, eventually made the bold decision to move from Iowa with her six-year-old daughter, Jane, to a small town, Claremont, in central New Hampshire, after divorcing her husband and leaving all that she owned in Iowa with her now ex-husband. This decision was extremely difficult for Sharon, but she had a more significant dream of meeting and being married to a man who truly loved her, accepted her for who she was, even with a young daughter from another man, and who would love her without conditions or requirements and not physically abuse her.

Sharon found a retail job in a clothing store on the main street in a nearby city, Newport, a close commute to her new hometown, Claremont, New Hampshire. After years of working, she met a handsome young and muscular man, Alex, the former star fullback on his high school football team, who had been forced to drop out of his high school after only two years when "The Great Depression" struck America and the world in 1929, resulting in, tragically and unexpectedly, both his parents losing their jobs concomitantly. This young, strong, muscular, and extremely self-confident male sophomore high school student and fullback of the football team, Alex, then was forced to make the difficult decision to quit high school, look for and find a job, and assist both his unemployed parents in paying the mortgage on their house so they would not become homeless. Alex, as a young and powerful man, was the first to find a job so that his parents could continue to pay their grocery bills, utility bills, and mortgage payments on their house each month. Alex found a job transporting ice blocks to his city neighbors for their ice boxes (these existed before modern refrigerators), located in the kitchen of all his neighbor's homes. He used metal ice tongs to pick up these very heavy blocks of ice, weighing 50 to 100 pounds per block, load them into his truck, drive to his customers' houses, then unload these same blocks from his truck and walk them up the sidewalk of each home and place these ice blocks into each home's kitchen and ice box.

After years of dating, Sharon and Alex fell deeply in love with each other. A dilemma existed, at least in their era of the 1920s in the United States of America, with regard to their relationship. Sharon grew up and was raised as a Methodist, Protestant, Christian woman. The man, Alex, whom she was now deeply in love with, was raised as a Catholic, Christian man. Sharon was now also divorced from her first and abusive husband. In the 1920s, it was considered taboo for a Catholic man to marry a divorced Protestant Christian woman.

Luckily, both individuals prioritized the power of their love for each other over political correctness and taboos existing in their era and decided to get married against and in opposition to the social norms existing in their era, which resulted in a very long, extremely rewarding, and amazing family and life for both Sharon and Alex! The deep, Holy, and genuine love Sharon and Alex had for each other was both recognized and acknowledged by God and their deep love for each other and their God, the same God for both Catholic and Protestant Christians, served as propitiation (for the societal taboo and their religious community members' resistance to a single unmarried Catholic Christian male marrying a divorced Protestant Christian female), for their blessed relationship and loving marriage that endured for the remainder of both their lives and throughout their future approach to centenarian status, and God further blessed their loving relationship with three additional children, including the fraternal twins, Judas and Ruth, and their younger brother, Thomas, who was born approximately six years after the twins were born!

Jane, the older step-sister to Ruth, was a wonderful and Godly woman, mentor, and supportive sister to Ruth. Throughout their childhood, because Jane was approximately six years older than Ruth, she was the ideal role model and mentor for her younger step-sister, henceforth or hereafter referred to as Ruth's older sister, a God-guided mentor and loving sister, because she was indeed and truly a benevolent person and a true "sister" in every sense of the word versus the more derogatory and unnecessary "detracting-of-glory" term that society typically labels as "step-sister."

Jane's virtue and many accomplishments and victories in showing her love for others in life are too numerous to delineate in one book without an infinite number of pages to write and be read by all who genuinely wish to know this Godly woman in the way that her younger sister knew and loved her older sister until God redeemed her older sister, after her mission of goodness had been completed on Earth, and fulfilled God's purpose for her on this planet and subsequently ensured her reservation and destiny to be fulfilled, as was God's intention for her, to attain and be honored with the highest exalted position and status in heaven at the right hand of "God The Father" (of her, her entire family and descendants, and, hopefully in the future, for all human beings on Earth, "God's children.")

Jane helped raise all her younger loving siblings and supported them unconditionally throughout their lives. Jane was a tremendous blessing to her mother, Sharon, who was busy working her entire life, alongside her loving and generous yet poor and meek husband. Jane's love and support for her mother as well as her siblings, from their birth and throughout grammar school, high school, university, and married lives, empowered and motivated her mother, Sharon, to change occupations, e.g., from a clothing retail store attendant occupation, to becoming the bookkeeper for the Dartmouth County School District in Dartmouth, New Hampshire. Sharon's transition to this new responsibility and occupation, though moderately inconvenient due to the required further daily commute to and from work for Sharon was, more importantly, a more difficult and intellectually challenging job or occupation and was a higher-paying occupation, which was, again, both more interesting, satisfying, and mentally challenging for Sharon, all aspects, characteristics, and features which Sharon desired, looked forward to, and welcomed with both arms. Sharon, like all her children, always desired and relished challenges in life that force you to learn and perform at an intellectual, spiritual, social, mental, and physical level that you might have thought you were not capable of, but nevertheless willing to take the chance and challenge to "raise your game" and elevate your performance to the highest level possible to not only achieve the required level of performance for that task or occupation, but to even far exceed the expectations that others have for you in the performance of that job or occupation. These priceless and ephemeral, God-guided work ethic and work attitudes were, by the blessing of God's guidance and Holy Spirit, passed down to all Sharon's children and future generations.

The parents, Sharon and Alex, of Jane, Ruth, Judas, and Thomas did their best to bring up all their children with a sense of meekness, humility, and God-fearing, God-respecting values, guidelines, perspectives, and aspirations in life. Thomas, the youngest male child, was appropriately named because, of all the children in the family, he always, from birth until death, doubted and outright denied the existence of God and the blessings that may derived by both accepting and acknowledging the presence of God as his creator and redeemer in his life journey, and suffered immeasurably from this perspective and attitude, which passed down to his children's generation, and, tragically, Thomas died years before all his elder siblings, none of whom were perfect, but believed in God and acknowledged God as their creator, and Jesus Christ not simply as their "propitiator" but the "propitiation." He, Jesus, is what satisfies the justice of God, and all Thomas's siblings, along with Thomas, were raised in the local Methodist church in Claremont, New Hampshire, yet only doubting Thomas failed to ever accept God as his creator, and Jesus Christ as his "propitiation."

Having somehow survived and navigated the dark, dreary, dull, drab, depressing, discouraging era of "The Great Depression" in the United States of America, which lasted ten years (some would say twenty or more years), after the 1929 stock market crash, which devastated many Americans and American businesses, resulting in mass unemployment and starvation of many people and families throughout America and the world, both parents, Sharon and Alex taught every single lesson they learned from their parents, who experienced the full and devastating impact of "The Great Depression" firsthand, to all their children, Jane, Ruth, Judas, and Thomas. For better or worse (always better in the God-inspired eyes of those children brought up in the Methodist church to love, honor, and respect God, Jesus Christ, and the Holy Spirit, otherwise known as the Holy Trinity), all children benefitted from the wise instruction and mentoring of their parents from birth to death, and all children respected their mother and father until their death and thereafter for the wonderful guidance they received, and the love both parents demonstrated to all their children.

Interestingly, though also sad, only the youngest child, "doubting [or rejecting] Thomas," failed to embrace God's grace, mercy, guidance, and Jesus Christ as the "propitiation." Thomas also neglected to accept the Holy Spirit's guidance of God in his life, from birth to death, even being so bold, though misinformed and misguided and truly evil, to write a manuscript endorsing "atheism." Despite the seventy years or more that Thomas was freely given the love of God via his parents and all his older siblings, Thomas fatefully rejected God in every instance of his life.

The post-depression era teachings that parents, Sharon and Alex passed on to their children daily throughout their upbringing, grammar school to high school to university, to married adult life, and thereafter, were many and priceless "to those who have ears to hear" (a phrase similar to: "to him who has ears to hear," a very specific reference to a phenomenal music album and theme song by a mighty and earth-changing vocalist and Christian musician named Keith Green). Keith Green, by the way, is not and would never, purposefully exclude those who are actually deaf from his timeless and earth-changing message to society, and the many positive and uplifting messages in his multiple, priceless and unmatched, life-changing songs contained in his endless list of albums that forever changed this Earth, before his untimely and premature death on a plane flight related to a missionary trip, in which he was again, doing his very best to be the most uplifting messenger of God on this Earth, to the best of his ability and as a truly inspiring individual who unfortunately, has not been appreciated or talked about enough (as he should be) on this planet, and in theis universe).

All these children learned terrific lessons that are impossible to dispute in life, such as: do not waste food, do not waste or foolishly spend money you worked hard and earnestly to honestly earn, be kind and respectful to your parents, your siblings, and everyone you encounter in your life, for you only have but one life in this universe and on this planet Earth, respect God in all your perspectives, attitudes, aspirations, and actions (and God will bless you via grace, mercy, compassion, and love despite your never being perfect enough or able to "earn" or merit this generous blessing, guidance, protection, salvation, and redemption from your sins, from and by God, Jesus Christ, and the Holy Spirit [also known as "The Holy Trinity", all equally representative of God]), and to avoid "worldly values [non-values], temptations, mind-altering, and mind/body-destroying chemicals and substances such as alcohol, tobacco, marijuana, cocaine, and other narcotics, magic mushrooms, LSD, methamphetamines, paint sniffing, huffing, and other devastating chemicals that might be addictive, life-destroying, mind/brain-damaging, and body-killing, in their final and ultimate consequences of repeated use (abuse or dependence often the sequela of initial use).

While Jane, Ruth, and Judas all revered their parents and their parents' wise advice and mentoring, which greatly benefitted all these siblings for the entirety of their lives, Thomas was, again, unfortunately, unwilling to heed this wise mentoring by his parents. Thomas, very enlightening to his siblings and descendants, just before his death, shed some light on how his attitudes, life perspectives, and ill-advised lifestyle had been adversely impacted and affected by some interesting events he experienced as a young child. Thomas stated "that, as a young child (and apparently for the remainder of his life), he resented the fact that he was not able to see his relatives and cousins as often as he would have liked to when growing up because of the rift and differences between Catholic Christians and Protestant Christians (e.g., Methodist, Presbyterian, Baptist), and, furthermore, because his Catholic background Christian father had married his previously-divorced Protestant background Christian mother."

This was a shocking revelation to all the family members of Thomas, his siblings, and all his family members, and all the descendants of Thomas and his siblings' descendants, for all of Thomas's siblings had experienced the era taboos and religion denomination differences and distinctions, some justified, some unjustified or unwarranted, yet had somehow ignored these negative or divisive aspects or revelations and simply moved on with their life, never doubting the existence of God, or God's omniscience, omnipresence, and omnipotence in their own lives. Thomas's parents, relatives, and siblings all chose to embrace God's guidance, protection, grace, mercy, compassion, and love wholeheartedly, resulting in lifelong, repeated blessings, and impressive accomplishments, and, perhaps most importantly, resilience in "dark, cruel, 'trying times' of fear, uncertainty, discouragement, disappointment" (with their own or others behavior around them), and to navigate through these dark passages and arrive at their ultimate destination of realizing that God is good and will never test them beyond their means to effectively and appropriately deal with, navigate through, and overcome such stressful and testing times, because, as their creator, God, only hopes, always, that his creations will acknowledge, worship, and accept the propitiation, known as Jesus Christ, the human form of God who suffered for the sins of all the less-than-perfect humans in this world, to pay for their sins, enabling all humans to be reunited in heaven with God forever.

Sharon and Alex, when their children were in grammar school and high school, masterfully demonstrated their love for all of God's human creations by opening their home to both impoverished individuals in the community, giving them an upstairs, separated room from the remainder of the house, to live in until they could find a job and live on their own, in addition to allowing all those in their small town and community to use their living room for funeral services, especially if and when they could not afford the more expensive funeral home services in town.

CHAPTER TWO

The Great Depression And The Everlasting
Teachings Both Sisters Learned From The Effect
On Their Parents Who Were Forced To Raise
Four Children With Depression Era Deficient
Income And Work Opportunities

Alex, after many years of working as an ice box stocker and ice
delivery man, and after having to withdraw from high school

after his second year or sophomore year of high school, to provide income for his parents whom both lost their jobs as a result of "The Great Depression," so his parents would not lose their home as a result of not being able to buy food for their family and make necessary monthly payments for their home mortgage, later found a job working at a machine shop, where his job was to punch holes in pieces of metal to manufacture various types of "metal washers." Touchingly, he kept this job for over 50 years, to ensure that his wife and children would be provided for, regardless of how long the after-effects of "The Great Depression" would last, and in the event that additional "Great Depressions" reappear suddenly and unexpectedly at any time in the future. Ruth's youngest son cried (tears from and for God) when he first heard this story.

Though Alex made very little money in this metalwork company job, which was a far commute from his hometown, and even in a different state, which Alex commuted to every weekday and on various weekends as well, Alex, being the supreme example of a God-respecting, God-guided mentor and role model for all his children, and generous without limits, sent all his children 5 dollars per month from his metal factory earnings and income, throughout all his children's entire educational careers, including graduate schools to obtain their doctoral degrees. Ruth's youngest son cried again after hearing these details. Is there anyone on this planet who would not be touched by this revelation of a parent's love for his children!

Thankfully, Alex's wife, as previously stated, at some point in her occupational career, transitioned from a retail clothing store sales agent to become the bookkeeper for Dartmouth

County School District in Dartmouth, New Hampshire, and eventually, she made more monthly income than her tireless, faithful, and hard-working husband, who as a result of what he saw as a teenager, when his parents both lost their jobs and were unable to find equivalent paying jobs thereafter for numerous years, due to the catastrophic and cataclysmic aftermath of the 1929 stock market crash in the United States of America and the subsequent "Great Depression," which lasted for more than a decade, was hesitant and reticent to ever leave his loyal employer, who, through tough times and good times, never intimated or ever suggested laying off Alex from his job, knowing that he had a wife and four children to feed and support.

As if this spellbinding account of the generosity of Alex as Christian man and a father of tremendous generosity toward his children, despite his meager job earnings, Alex was the most consistent and generous sender of small dollar amount birthday checks to every single (many in total) grandchild of his, including Ruth's youngest son. Most grandchildren were clueless as to the importance of this act of kindness by their grandfather, having no idea how little money their grandfather actually earned at his job each week and month at his workplace. Sadly, as often occurs, only after Alex's death did most of his grandchildren learn just how little money he earned in his life, yet displayed the generosity of a six-figure professional worker in the manner and practice he had of sending all his children and grandchildren gift checks throughout their education student years and post-graduate years, and on their birthdays. If you have not already surmised on your own what a magnificently generous, humble, hard-working, and magnificent father, grandfather, and Godly

Christian mentor was to all his descendants, then let me reassure you that he was indeed, "The Man In The Arena," and an unbelievable man of God, in both his teachings and actions, each and every day of his life.

Many years later in Alex's life, he was informed by his wife's physician that his wife Sharon had been diagnosed with Alzheimer's disease. For the next twenty-plus years, Alex faithfully loved his wife, the love of his life, and never even contemplated "abandoning this sinking ship," as many other humans have done, in the experience of this observer. As Alex's wife's memory of life events slowly receded, initially, then later, near the end of her life, even included intermittent memory deficits about who the man was that came to her room every day and spent breakfast and lunch with her. Alex was heartbroken but had the strength of God's love in his quiver to deliver as many Valentine's Day arrows of love to his ailing wife as was necessary every day to both show his love for his Godly wife and to acknowledge his respect for and love of God, who had blessed him in so many ways by leading him to meet and marry this amazing woman whom God also blessed by introducing her to Alex, her human equivalent of God's love for Sharon.

For the twenty-plus years of Alex's wife's disease, Alex was kind, understanding, forgiving, and made every effort on this Earth that he could imagine to help her and to let her see, interact with, and communicate with all their children, grandchildren, and great-grandchildren. Alex bought a Winnebago and would drive from Claremont, New Hampshire to Connecticut or California to visit all his children and their families whenever possible during summer or winter, as coordinated and arranged with his children's permission to visit, and would stay several weeks or months, with each of his children's families at different times, to allow his wife, Sharon, to have life-enhancing and loving interactions and communications with their mother. Alex was also a legend and master card game man and taught all his children and grandchildren how to be masters of their card-playing games universe.

Alex and his wife Sharon did everything within their powers to also attend every and all their children's and grandchildren's or great grandchildren's graduations, weddings, and other special life achievement events or receptions where any relatives were receiving various honors or accolades.

In the cases of several grandchildren, Alex and his wife Sharon attended the grammar school graduations where both their grandchildren graduated at the top of their class, then the high school graduations where both grandchildren graduated at the top of their class, and then the college and graduate school graduations where their grandchildren graduated, once again, at the top of their classes. The unwavering love and support of relatives and friends in this world is perhaps God's greatest gift to less-than-perfect humans, and is exceeded only by God's compassion, grace, mercy, and love in allowing Jesus Christ as the propitiation.

CHAPTER THREE

Even though Alex was raised by Catholic Christian parents and grew up going to Catholic Christian masses every Sunday, when he married Sharon, they agreed to raise the children in the local Claremont, New Hampshire Methodist and Protestant Christian church. Jane, Ruth, Judas, and Thomas were all taken to their local Methodist church every Sunday by their parents, Sharon and Alex. In the neighborhood that these children grew up in, all the neighbors attended various churches, including the Catholic, Methodist, Presbyterian, and Lutheran denominations.

By attending church each Sunday with their parents, the children in their community all grew up with keen wisdom and insight, and became responsible children, teenagers, and adults as a result of their weekly church attendance and enlightening life principles and guidelines that were espoused by their church pastors (life mentors) from the earliest ages imaginable. This experience was priceless and invaluable to all these community children, enabling them to be leaders for the rest of their lives. They all developed fantastic leadership skills and were guided by their moral, ethical, social, physical routines that they learned very early in their life during children's bible school and later, during sermons in the main church. One may ask what physical routines or principles can be taught to and learned by children raised in the church? Such principles, found in the Bible, include, among many others, the teachings that your body is your temple and God, your creator's temple, simultaneously and concomitantly, and a second principle is that you run a race to win, not just to finish the race. The implications and suggestions in these two principles in the Bible are that you are to maintain a healthy and strong body (God's temple and your temple that you honor God with), and you are encouraged by

God to train and prepare for "races in life" (e.g., any endeavors and challenges you encounter), with great attention to planning, preparation, and strategic training to perform at your best every day (e.g., God's desire for all his human creations is that they run each of their individual life journeys, also known as "races," with the attitude, perspective, aspiration to perform at their very best each day to win their "race" every day of their lives).

Jane and Ruth were both irresistibly cute young girls growing up in the small city and community of Claremont, New Hampshire (confirmed many years later by their male and female classmates from grammar school and high school, at the 40, 45, and 50 year reunions, while riding together on their class year parade floats, repeatedly saying that both young girls were, from their male classmates, their dream girlfriends, even if not in reality, and their female classmates, who stated that both young girls were the leaders of their classes, by life example, via their humility and meekness, yet proactive class members, both having filled the entire yearbook accomplishments square, under their senior class photos, with so many different sports teams, scholarships awarded, and leadership roles that their description boxes were filled with multiple paragraphs versus several words or lines of activities seen under the pictures of the majority of their loving and supportive classmates.

Despite Jane and Ruth's proactive, humble, meek, yet prolific and dynamic volunteer leadership roles in many different sports (e.g., basketball, field hockey, track and field, dance competitions (winning most if not all of these competitions), and other sports), grammar school and high school club leadership roles, and scholarships earned that paid for most of their eventual university tuition bills after their high school graduation with academic honors, both Jane and Ruth earned the respect, love, and admiration of all their classmates by their daily habits of showing humility, kindness, exceptional proactive listening skills (especially with regard to all their various classmates' everyday concerns, fears, anxieties, or depression), and responding to their classmates with attitudes, perspectives, aspirations, and actions of benevolence, based on Godly Christian principles that they learned every Sunday in their Methodist church services. The males on the class reunion floats repeatedly spoke of both Jane and Ruth as their "ideal dream date women," which they fantasized about when they were, e.g., the star pitcher on the grammar school and high school baseball team or the starting running back on the high school football team, or the most intelligent male student in the classes which either Jane or Ruth were members of and actively involved in multiple significant leadership roles as well as club members.

As the children of both Jane and Ruth, on the reunion floats with their mothers, hearing these stories was both entertaining and surprising, as both these women failed to brag or boast about their many grammar school and high school achievements, but chose rather to move on, look forward (instead of backward), both becoming outstanding, A+ grade mothers to their multiple children, who again, were privileged to hear these lovely stories about their mothers at these 40-year, 45-year, and 50-year high school reunions!

Even more impressive, at least to the descendants or children of these "Two Sisters, The Dynamic Duo, Pilgrimage to Eternity," was the confirmation of the respect and honor that both these young girls received from their classmates when reviewing the grammar school and high school yearbooks that were brought to all their reunion gatherings in Claremont, New Hampshire. Unlike most larger cities where children may have had multiple distinct grammar schools and high schools to attend, Claremont had a grammar school and a high school, so that everyone grew up with and knew everyone from very young ages. The myriad kind inscriptions made in the yearbooks of both Jane and Ruth was overwhelmingly positive and kind, with unlimited best wishes directed to both Jane and Ruth, when these "Dynamic Duo Sisters" both eventually departed Claremont, New Hampshire, upon graduating from high school, to explore and pursue their university education in California, United States of America. You have no idea how proud the children of these "Two Sisters, The Dynamic Duo," were when they heard all these stories of how kind, popular, loved, and respected their mothers were when they were young sisters in grammar school and high school, and how all their male student classmates had wanted them to be their girlfriends, but they never had this wish fulfilled because both daughters were too focused on their academic studies, sports team participation, club and student leadership roles throughout their early education years, to consider any marked or serious opposite-sex romantic relationships, before attending university studies in California, after both sister's graduation from high school in Claremont, New Hampshire. One such example was when the son of Ruth learned that his mother was the most energetic and unstoppable guard on the high school basketball team, even though his mother had never even informed him that she played high school basketball! The same son also learned, only at the reunion parade while accompanying his mother on the 40-year high school reunion class float, that his mother had been voted by her classmates to receive the honor of senior class "Prom Queen," known as a great honor by her son. Again, the son of Ruth was shocked and amazed by his mother's humility in never having even mentioned this honor to him or his older brother.

That was just who Ruth, his mother, was: a kind, humble, thankful person who neither desired nor required constant compliments for her many amazing accomplishments throughout her life, but instead sought to always look forward and not backward, which enabled her to continuously perform her best each day of her life, which both of her sons could absolutely verify, because she not only excelled in everything she endeavored to accomplish in life, such as motherhood, but she also taught both her sons to have the exact same life perspective that she learned while growing up in the church and passed all her wise teachings on to her next generation, namely both her sons. Her two sons honored her and benefitted immensely from her enlightenment, and both learned from their mother how to be kind, humble, and meek, yet super achievers in every task and endeavor they pursued, all God-guided and God-directed endeavors, goals, aspirations, and amazing life achievements. Just to give a tip of the iceberg clue of how this dynamic girl, then mature mother, forever guided and blessed both her sons with her teachings of wisdom from A to Z, focused always on goals and activities motivated and inspired by teachings in the Bible, both her sons became prominent leaders in their grammar schools and high schools, and both sons were the number one, e.g., "valedictorian," student academically in their high school, and were similarly, in the past, the top students in their grammar school graduating classes. Additionally, both sons competed in multiple sports in both grammar school and high school, and qualified for the "Junior Olympics" in grammar school, and were top athletes and "Academic All-Americans" in high school. In addition, both her sons, as a result of her constant kindness, caring, loving, teaching, and uplifting attitudes and Christian perspectives, became professional musicians as grammar school students and received college scholarships and "Honors at Entrance" at their selected universities. These blessings from a dynamic mother also led to doctorate studies being completed with the highest academic honors and achievements imaginable, all the result of a truly loving, kind, and God-gifted wise, and dynamic mother!

Ruth's older sister, Jane, was a similar miraculous blessing to her entire family and all four of her children. Jane, after graduating from high school, pursued pre-medicine university studies at the University of Southern California (USC University, as is known to local Southern California residents). While successfully completing her "pre-medicine" classes, she met an amazing, kind man, Sam, who had received a full scholarship to Pepperdine University, located in Malibu, CA, also in Southern California, and not far from USC, where Jane was completing her pre-medicine courses. You can guess what happened shortly after these two individuals met.

Jane married Sam, and they, shortly thereafter, had four children, Tim, Lisa, Lena, and Jacob over the next ten years! Jane taught all the God-guided, God-gifted enlightenment she had been gracefully and mercifully been endowed with as a result of her being brought up and raised in the Methodist Church in Claremont, New Hampshire, to all her children and blessed her husband with her kind spirit, love, and respect that she showed for her loving husband and all their four children. All four children advanced through their grammar school and high school with successful completion of their education and graduation with various distinctions, depending on which of the four children that you wish to focus on and explore their unique and individual talents, skills, qualities, and unique personalities.

The oldest son of Jane, Tim, as an American college football team member and "field goal kicker," successfully kicked a sixty-four-yard field goal, a feat (no pun intended for 'feet'), accomplished by only a select few individuals on this earth! This same eldest son of Jane later would marry "Miss California" beauty pageant winner (of questionable value or detriment in later years), then proceeded to become a fantastic general construction contractor and builder of homes, a vintage and classic sports car collector, a spiritual leader in his large Orange County, CA church, and a fantastic father to his own three daughters, up until the very last day and the last second of his God-blessed life!

Lisa was Tim's younger sister (the older sister of Tim's two sisters), by two years, and was also a dynamic woman who was blessed by God with masterful mothering skills and qualities, and had two daughters and one son. Each of her children was unique and special, and she raised them along with her husband, consistently demonstrating the most love possible at all times, enabling each of her three children to be the best they could be in life and excel in all their endeavors to the greatest extent possible, skills and qualities that extended to their own eventual families of future generations.

Lena, Jane's youngest daughter, similarly found the love of her life after high school, got married, and had three children of her own. Again she passed down the traits and personal qualities, and enlightenment principles taught to her by her mother, of Jane to her own three children. Her oldest daughter, along with Lena herself, became United States championship-level horse riders and competed in the National Championships for many years together. Her older of two sons had a passion for golf, along with his father, and excelled in this sport. Lena's youngest son was a most adventurous young man and had unlimited future potential to achieve his goals and dreams!

Jane's youngest son, Jacob, was a star athlete in grammar school and high school in baseball and basketball. He attended the same junior high school that his father, the former Pepperdine University full scholarship star basketball athlete, was the superintendent of, and together they led the basketball teams to championship games each year of attendance at this junior high school. He later found the ultimate, true love of his life, his wife, with whom he spent the entirety of his happy marriage, after a long and winding path, with many "ups and downs," to find his true love and soulmate, with whom he could then joyfully spend the later half of his life. He passed on what he learned from his mother, Jane, to his children and the next generation, which will forever favorably impact future generations of Jane and Sam's family.

CHAPTER FOUR

The Background Of The Dynamic Duo Sisters'
Parents And How This Background Led To
Unifying (More Than Divisive) Life Perspectives
And Positively Impacted The Upbringing Of
Their Children With, Luckily, A Rare Exception

Sharon and Alex, the parents of Jane and Ruth, e.g., "Two
Sisters, The Dynamic Duo," and Judas and Jacob grew up in

very diverse environments and with different backgrounds, yet their eventual acquaintance, deep and profound love and respect for each other, and marriage union culminated in a perfect blend of values which they were able to successfully bestow on all of their children, yet one of their children veered far and wide off the path his parents intended, hoped, and wished for him. This child was their youngest child, Jacob.

Sharon grew up in Iowa with the traditional "Little House on the Prairie" television show-like values, all based on the Holy Bible and American Constitution and American "Bill of Rights" principles and values, which focus on treating others with kindness, respect, equality in worth, and potential to achieve "The American Dream" on their own via earnest and hard work each day to strive toward their "well-thought-out" God-guided attitudes, aspirations, life goals, achievements, and accomplishments throughout their life and up until the day of their eventual physical death and spiritual resurrection to be with God, their creator, in heaven forever! Sharon grew up in the Methodist Church, whose origin was largely founded by and based on the life of John Wesley. Methodism, an 18th-century movement founded by John Wesley, sought to reform the Church of England from within. John Wesley (June 17, 1703– March 2, 1791) was an English cleric, theologian, and evangelist who was a leader of a revival movement within the Church of England known as Methodism. On February 28, 1784, John Wesley chartered the first Methodist Church in the United States.

Even though he was an Anglican, Wesley saw the need to provide church structure for his followers after the Anglican

Church abandoned its American believers during the American Revolution. The societies he founded became the dominant form of the independent Methodist movement that continues to this day. John Wesley was a Methodist traveling preacher, organizer of the Methodist Conference, and founder of the Methodist Church. After his conversion in 1738, he dedicated himself to promoting "vital" and "practical" religion and to preserving and increasing the life of God in men's souls.

John Wesley's most famous quote, and this quote defines both the background and upbringing of both parents, Sharon and Alex, even though Sharon grew up as a Protestant Christian and Alex grew up as a Catholic Christian, follows below:

> "Do all the good you can, by all the means you can, in all the ways you can, in all the places you can, at all the times you can, to all the people you can, as long as ever you can."

What is the current and unfortunate difference between Wesleyan and Methodist churches currently? Both trace their origins to John Wesley, whose enlightenment is the basis of their faith. However, the Wesleyans tend to be more conservative, centering on the church covenants and personal behavior of the members. The United Methodists are decidedly more liberal. What is the difference between Methodists and Wesleyans? They are part of a larger schism within other mainline Protestant denominations (namely, Episcopalians and Baptists), ostensibly over the propriety of same-sex marriage and the ordination of

LGBTQ clergy, though in reality, over a broader array of cultural touchpoints involving sexuality, gender, and religious pluralism.

What is causing the split in the Methodist church? More than 6,000 United Methodist congregations— a fifth of the U.S. total— have now received permission to leave the denomination amid a schism over theology and the role of LGBTQ people in the nation's second-largest Protestant denomination, as of July, 2023.

The merger in 1968 that formed the United Methodist Church brought together the Methodist Church, primarily of British background, and the Evangelical United Brethren Church, primarily of German background but very similar to the Methodists. Why are United Methodist churches disaffiliating? While the church forbids the marriage or ordination of "self-avowed, practicing homosexuals," many churches and conferences defy those bans. This prompted more conservative congregations to leave the denomination, as of July, 2023.

Alex grew up with a background and church affiliation directly associated with the Catholic church and Catholicism in the United States of America. His ancestors were of French origin and migrated first from France to Quebec, Canada, then migrated South into the New England region of the United States of America, specifically arriving to Claremont, New Hampshire. All his relatives were devout Catholics and attended Catholic church services every weekend and participated in other various Catholic gatherings scheduled on various weekdays and weeknights when their work schedules allowed their participation in these other gatherings during the work week.

Thomas, Alex and Sharon's youngest child, was approximately six years younger than his older fraternal twins, Ruth and Judas, and grew up in a slightly more isolated and lonely environment, specifically with regard to not having as many similar-aged friends or siblings around to interact and communicate with daily when he was growing up. Thomas's isolation and loneliness as a child was in stark contrast to his eldest sister, Jane, who always had the opportunity to engage in multiple conversations and other social interactions with her younger fraternal twins, who were only four years younger than Jane, and thus overlapped in attending the same grammar school and high school concomitantly with her younger twin siblings.

Perhaps this resulted in closer ties and family bonds between Jane and her twin siblings than with her youngest brother, who was ten years younger and thus attended school with a completely different group of school colleagues and classmates, almost a separate generation in both age and, perhaps, in the future, generational mindset and perspective on life principles and religious values, as it turned out, at least in Thomas's life story.

Although all four siblings grew up in the same home and presumably with the same parental guidance and mentoring of both wise, reverent, and Godly parents, Alex and Sharon, somehow Thomas's life journey would be navigated through much more uncertain and "The Perfect Storm" turbulent waves to arrive at his final destination of a somewhat shorter than expected and a less positive and fulfilling life than he anticipated and expected, along with his wife and children.

What dynamics were most relevant and applicable to Thomas's life attitudes, perspectives, aspirations, and goals, all of which, sadly and disappointing as they were, adversely impacted both his longevity and ability to optimally motivate, inspire, energize, and mentor his work and social network colleagues, family members, and all others around him who were interacting with him daily, to the greatest extent possible? To describe one all-important, essential, and life-enhancing element that Thomas was missing in his life and that was having a devastating impact on him and his view of the world as a result of this missing element, in a single word, Thomas lacked: "God." Thomas's doubting attitude, lack of trust, lack of faith in God, lack of purpose and benevolent direction for his life journey distorted his life view. This resulted in a chaotic and convoluted, highly uncertain, unfocused, negative perspective regarding all of life's challenges, and no self-confidence, that only comes with the strength, safety, protection, and reassurance a human derives from placing all their insecurities, anxiety, depression, and discouragement in the loving hands of God who is always, twenty-four hours a day, receptive of these life burdens, and who replaces them with the human versions of God's omniscience, omnipotence, and omnipresence, making each God-revering human more of a superhuman without limits than a non-Godly human who is forever burdened with the limitations of his birth and future life, dependent solely on his isolated and lonely existence, a very depressing scenario indeed.

While Jane, Ruth, and Judas, for the most part, were always smiling, positive, encouraging, motivating, and inspiring to all those around them every day of their lives, Thomas chose as a young child to reject God in his life, and never agreed or submitted to changing this belief as an adult. This abysmal decision by Thomas to insist that there is no God in his life, or the world, or in this universe, or in other universes, undoubtedly led to his untimely and premature death. Thomas experienced a horror movie-like existence, whereby he always looked at and treated others with the same negative life perspective that he, unjustly and unadvisedly, chose for himself. At Thomas's funeral, numerous people who were business clients and customers of Thomas's business, and who had no relationship to and had never met the relatives of Thomas who attended his funeral, openly and inappropriately divulged stories to Thomas's siblings and other relatives of how Thomas made multiple statements, inappropriate jokes, and sexually harassing or intimidating comments during the many years that Thomas worked with or on projects with his customers and clients over the entirety of his professional career. Thomas's relatives were devastated to hear these negative feedback remarks from business clients of Thomas, who agreed to attend his funeral, despite these business colleagues or business customers' depressing, negative, and resentful feelings toward Thomas and his multiple inappropriate remarks, attitudes, perspectives, and actions for the entire duration of his professional career.

While Thomas lived a tumultuous life, from childhood, through his teenage years, into his adult professional life, and until the last day of his finite life and premature, unexpected sudden death, the positive aspects that all his loving siblings and relatives must now focus on and remember forever is that he was blessed in several aspects of his life, including his marriage to a like-minded wife, and that he was blessed with two children, boys, approximately three years separated in their age, who, despite not having an ideal, God-loving father and mother, advanced through school and life to the best of their non-God-guided ability, but not without unfortunate and misguided directions taken by both sons, as a result of the poor mentoring both sons received by both parents who knew of God, but openly rejected God in their lives and the lives of both their sons.

Thomas and his wife, Monica, whom he met in graduate school, both indulged freely and openly in all the evil vices and actions of their era, the 1960's and 1970's, while college and graduate school participants. They both drank all types of alcohol and participated in all types of various illicit drug abuse of their era, again due to the lack of God in both their lives. Their second child was born with a severe condition requiring multiple surgeries, and was always, rightly or unjustly, suspected as a possible consequence or sequela to either the mother's continued abuse of alcohol and drugs before, during, and after her pregnancy and possibly also due to Thomas's continued abuse of alcohol and drugs before, during, and after his wife's pregnancy. Devastating to all of Thomas's family members and siblings, who engaged in no such substance abuse, was the revelation that Thomas and his wife, Monica, probably negatively influenced both their sons to also engage in similar alcohol and drug abuse, but even worse, their influence might have also tempted and corrupted Thomas's oldest sister's children, two in total, namely Jane's youngest daughter, Lena, and youngest son, Jacob, to begin drinking while they were in grammar school and high school. Both children later developed into raging alcoholics as young and middle-aged adults, which eventually destroyed their initial marriages and had a devastating impact on their spouses and children. Lena's three children and Jacob's two children were adversely impacted by their parent's alcoholism, and the poor decision-making, labile mood swings, and irresponsible behavior that inevitably follows those who become addicted to and dependent on the brain and body poison known as "alcohol." Both Lena, after a near-death experience from alcoholism and divorce by her husband, and Jacob, after losing his first two wives and marriages to drug and alcohol abuse, eventually, and after approximately three inpatient drug and alcohol rehabilitation programs were completed by both Lena and Jacob, they were saved by God's grace and mercy, and both individuals continued their sobriety now, hopefully, in Jacob's case, with his third and final wife, and for both, recovering families and children who can forgive their parents for becoming addicted to mind-destroying and body-destroying alcohol, tobacco, and illicit substance abuse (e.g., marijuana abuse, methamphetamines abuse, lysergic acid abuse, paint sniffing, huffing, magic mushrooms abuse, fentanyl, and narcotics abuse, benzodiazepines abuse, myriad other abused illicit drugs, and abuse of prescribed drugs).

"The cup is always half or more full, and never half or more empty." This dogma or philosophy should be embraced by all humans on this planet. Believing in God makes this perspective easy and automatic. Despite the negativity and realism of the above disheartening paragraphs relating true experiences in the lives of real people on this Earth, all persons must never lose sight of the fact that prudent, Godly decisions and choices at the earliest age possible in life, including repenting of one's sins and abusive, manipulative, evil behavior presently or in the past, can always be performed by every human on Earth, regardless of their age, to turn one's life around and head in a direction 180 degrees opposite of the detrimental decisions and life that one was living the moment before their enlightened decision to choose faith in God to redirect their life and redeem them from their past iniquities and sinful behavior!

CHAPTER FIVE

The Astonishing Impact Of "The Great Depression" On The Importance Of Occupation, Loyalty To Employers, And Job Security On Both Parents And The Everlasting Wisdom Bestowed On All The Siblings And Descendants Of "The Dynamic Duo" Two Sisters

"The Great Depression" was anything but great. Its disheartening, dire, and inevitable impact forever changed the manner in which an entire generation of humans learned, interpreted, and then responded to this crisis, and most importantly, passed on the painful learning and wisdom they acquired by persevering and surviving this problematic era, which, in essence, can be summarized by the following statement and life philosophy: "One must always be positive, resilient, indestructible, hard-working, and refuse to be defeated. Despite periods of no food, no money to pay daily and monthly bills, and no money to spoil and splurge in spending for oneself or one's children, there are indeed many priceless life lessons that one may learn by navigating this storm and staying afloat despite the near-drowning that this hurricane inflicted on the world." Essentially, every life lesson learned during "The Great Depression" by its survivors, by God's grace, could and were passed down to the next generation, e.g., their children, directly through their daily communications with their family and indirectly via the children observing the stress and hardship their parents were going through and forever remembering that, though times were seemingly hopeless in many instances, their parents always, miraculously, gave thanks to God for what they had each day, rather than obsessing negatively on what they did not have, or what their neighbors had and they were lacking, thus, this entire generation of "The Great Depression" survivors learned what is important in life and how to navigate perilous storms to arrive at their desired destination, their loving and supportive family, every day and night.

This generation of parents and children also learned that though it might be true that their lives are mere fleeting moments in eternity, nevertheless, all human lives are important, and when endangered, whether it be from frustration, job loss, inability to find work, inability to keep or find a home or afford a place to rent and live, anxiety, depression, anger, or rage, that all human beings, in these circumstances, can and should be supportive of each other as fellow human beings and equally valued members of God's family. Ironically, and sadly, generations who are fortunate enough to never experience or undergo trials of tremendous stress which pushed individuals of that generation to their limits of responsibility, resilience, and endurance, to navigate tremendous and perilous storms, e.g., World War I, World War II, Korean War, Vietnam War, and others, are likely to be most vulnerable and the least resilient, when tough times do come, resulting in inexplicable and inappropriate responses to even minor stressful situations. No one, including this author, would ever suggest or recommend that wars or "The Great Depression" are required or recommended to make more humans resilient, more supportive, more compassionate, more loving, and better family members of God; however, this does occur in intermittent generation-skipping eras, which, thankfully, allows continuity of and passing on of life-changing and life-enhancing human values and characteristics to each generation, even if it must come from two generations before a particular generation, most in need of these redeeming, priceless mentors and role models of human compassion and resilience. Qualities honed and perfected in brutal eras include courage, ignoring and suppressing thoughts or inclinations of cowardice, taking on "Man in the Arena" volunteer roles and responsibilities when vital, necessary, or required for the betterment of society and mankind, and resolve to start a task, work endlessly, and with an undefeatable attitude to complete that task with the most incredible precision, accuracy, and professionalism to achieve unparalleled success in the final product or outcome of the original task taken on voluntarily or assigned to that individual, to help many others who are not as capable or qualified to complete the task. These principles are the keys to making every society better for every human being within each society, regardless of whatever chaos is occurring in a specific generation or era.

Alex, when his parents lost both their jobs during "The Great Depression," boldly and immediately came to their rescue, e.g., as the "Man in the Arena" dropped out of high school after his sophomore year (second year of high school), went out and looked for a job, found the only job he could find and was qualified for, as the star fullback football player on his high school football team, picking up tremendously heavy ice blocks with heavy steel tongs, and transporting these ice blocks from the ice company that hired him, to the homes of everyone in his hometown and surrounding towns in order to ensure that his parents, who were both older and weaker and could never successfully complete this ice block delivery job, could continue to pay their home mortgage payment, utility bills, trash bills, have money to feed themselves and their children, and continue to tithe (give 10% of their earnings) to their local church, which would then use this money to support community members who were even more impoverished or in more desperate need or in more dire circumstances than Alex's parents and family.

Alex later transitioned to a metal manufacturing company job in the neighboring state of Vermont, which he commuted to each day from Claremont, New Hampshire, each work day, a job that he held for over fifty years, all to ensure that his own family, including his wife, Sharon, and their four children, Jane and Ruth (Two Sisters, "The Dynamic Duo"), Judas, and Thomas never had to experience the tremendous hardship, anxiety, depression, discouragement, discomfort, and overwhelming fears that life as they had known would never return to "normal" after the 1929 United States of America stock market crash and "The Great Depression" that ensued and continued for ten years (some would say twenty or more years), before anyone could honestly say that life had "returned to normal," that Alex and his family experienced and had to endure!

Alex and Sharon both taught all their children that the food on their plate, whether it be for breakfast, lunch, or dinner, was always to be eaten in its entirety, and never to be wasted. While modern nutritionists might argue that is a recipe for the development of obesity, this concept was irrelevant with regard to "The Great Depression" generation and in the "post-Great Depression" generation or era, also known as the children of "The Great Depression," adults who survived this tremendous era of stress and uncertainty.

Remember, many suicides occurred during and in the decade (s) after "The Great Depression" by those who humans without God in their heart, soul, and mind, every minute of every hour, day, week, month, and for many years after the 1929 stock market crash. Two generations later, the descendants of our entire family still never waste any food and never take food for granted or guaranteed availability. We all recognize and realize, based on the repeated teachings and wise instructions from our parents that not everyone can afford food to eat every day, and when we receive food that someone else has purchased and prepared for us, we are never to decline or waste that edible food, unless an extraordinary circumstance exists whereby the food is unsafe, dangerous, or deleterious in some way or another, of course.

All descendants were taught the value and responsibility of all humans to also be open to recycling, as this was good for the community and earth. Whether it be aluminum cans, glass bottles, or cardboard, when Ruth's children were growing up without money, Ruth educated, encouraged, and enlightened both her very young boys to collect all three of these items whenever possible and store them in the recycling bins in the car garage, and then, on specified Saturdays, we would load the recycling bins into a vehicle and deliver the bins to the recycling company that would weigh each bin, and pay both boys a small amount of money, the recycling fee due, to reward both boys for their recycling efforts each month, and provide them with some income for occasional candy bars or treats or drinks safe for children. This recycling regimen was definitely a "post-Great Depression" and "earth-improving practice" that Ruth learned from her upbringing and parents, which she passed on or taught to her children for their benefit and for the benefit of her local community and society.

As previously mentioned, Sharon worked for many years in a retail clothing store on the main street in her hometown, and also in neighboring towns when other jobs and working hours were made available, all to support and provide income, food, pay education expenses, and pay other family expenses necessary and required for her four beautiful and Godly children and husband. Not all women worked back in the 1920s and 1930s, yet Sharon was the "Woman in the Arena," shunning nonsense taboos or norms of her era and focusing, rightly so, on providing the best family experience, education, happiness for her family, which required her to work, and every family member benefitted from her bold willingness to support and ensure that all her family members were well-provided for. These traits of boldness, proactiveness, practicality, being a team player, and unwavering support, love, understanding, grace, mercy, gratitude, and desire to ensure that all her children had education supplies and food they needed for school and studying effectively and efficiently at home, defined Sharon's greatness, and did not go unnoticed by her two daughters, the "Two Sisters, The Dynamic Duo." Later in Sharon's life, when her children were older and generating higher education expenses in high school and preparing to attend out-of-state state universities in California and Florida, Sharon applied for and was accepted and hired to work as a bookkeeper for the Dartmouth, New Hampshire county school district, and thereby earn an incremental amount of cash each year to better provide for the higher educational expenses her four children were incurring. This job was a significantly more intense job and a much further commute, being nowhere near Claremont, New Hampshire, where Sharon lived, however, none of these factors mattered to Sharon, because she felt the extra income was necessary and would be beneficial to both her husband and children and would add to the overall happiness and potential opportunities for her family members to enjoy better vacations but more importantly, apply to more universities and be accepted to higher education programs that they could pursue after graduating from high school. Sharon's dreams and aspirations all came true!

All four children of Sharon and Alex performed very well in grammar school, and high school, and all were accepted into quality universities, upon graduating from high school. Jane was accepted at the University of Southern California (USC), Ruth was accepted at San Jose State University in California, Judas was accepted into the University of California Berkeley, and Thomas was accepted at the University of Florida, then transferred to the University of California Los Angeles (UCLA).

Jane, being the amazing and dynamic woman she was, offered to lodge all three of her younger siblings in her home, along with her new husband and three children, when they first arrived in California and were preparing to attend their respective universities. A very loving, kind, generous woman and sister indeed! Jane was also a second mother to the future two children of her younger sister, Ruth, who several years later also married and established her own loving family, upon graduating from her university. Jane attended every single graduation ceremony of both children of her younger sister, Ruth, and every wedding as well. Jane would also take both boys of her younger sister to various pools, beaches, and children's entertainment parks in Orange County, California, and even San Diego, including among many other events and sites, Disneyland, Knott's Berry Farm, Laguna Beach, CA, Newport Beach, CA, Dana Point, CA, Sea World in San Diego, The San Diego Zoo, and others. Jane and Ruth truly loved and respected each other for the entirety of their lives and thus loved each other's children as if they were their very own children. Not a single child of these two women would ever even think of denying this fact, as they felt so much love from both these two sisters and all the children of these women also knew that both these women would one day continue to practice and perfect their loving mother traits and skills in heaven, after each of their children were successful, mature adults who were independent and living life to the fullest, God-blessed, possible extent. These women were honestly and truly God-blessed and God-inspired supremely generous and loving mothers to all their families and children, regardless and irrespective of what was going on around them and never insisted on or demanded others to behave at the immeasurable high level and standard that they operated at daily. In summary, they were the most qualified and loving mentors any children and family could hope for and imagine, and all their children knew that they would reunite and see them in heaven in the future as a result of their miraculous and God-inspired magnificent behavior and performance as optimal mentors and mothers on Earth, once in a generation, "Two Sisters, The Dynamic Duo, Pilgrimage to Eternity."

CHAPTER SIX

Dynamic Duo Sisters' University Era Of Healthy Living, Healthy Lifestyle, Learning And Perfecting Acts Of Kindness, Selfless And Altruistic Behavior, Acknowledging the Mercy They Received, Maximizing Their Acquisition Of Wisdom, And Gracefully And Humbly Accepting And Being Thankful For This Era And "Age Of Enlightenment" In Their Lives

Jane, the oldest daughter of Alex and Sharon, was accepted, after high school graduation at Stevens High School (this high school has the longest active and uninterrupted annual high school reunion record in the United States), for admission into the University of Southern California (USC) for her undergraduate college education as a premedical student. She had a fantastic experience in college making many friends among her classmates and learning that happiness in life is not just making yourself happy but making yourself and everyone you interact with and communicate with happy, content, safe, confident, supported, encouraged, motivated, inspired, and enlightened with God's teachings from the Bible, the greatest book ever written.

When you make these your goals and aspirations and motivation in your life, you transform yourself from an ordinary and average person into a dynamic and transformational person with regard to yourself and all those other humans you encounter and interact with every day of your life until your physical death and spiritual life continuance onto and into eternity, under the auspices, protection, and the direction of God your Father and Creator. Jane, in addition to being a fantastic premedical education student during her USC University experience, also was blessed by God to meet her future husband and future father of her four children, two boys, and two girls. Jane and her husband met during their college years and were married shortly after graduating from their respective universities, Jane of USC University in Los Angeles, CA, and her husband, a university scholarship star basketball player, recruited as a star high school basketball player from Branson, Missouri, at Pepperdine University in Malibu, California.

Jane, in addition to completing her university studies, was a phenomenal dancer and became a dance instructor at the University of Southern California (USC), and also taught her younger fraternal twin siblings, Judas and Ruth, to be (similar to herself) phenomenal dancers and dance partners, to the extent that her younger fraternal twin siblings then went on to win almost all the dance competitions they participated in throughout the entire New England region of the East Coast of the United States of America.

Jane's husband, Miles, graduated from Pepperdine University and became the Superintendent of a junior high school (grades 7, 8, and 9; approximately ages 12 years old to 14 years old students), in Anaheim, CA, a short drive from his alma mater, Pepperdine University, to Anaheim in Orange County, California. Jane's youngest son would later become a star guard basketball player at the very same junior high school where her husband was Superintendent! This same son, mid-way through his basketball stardom would suffer an inconvenient and unfortunate accident whereby he accidentally cut off the distal third of one finger during his "Wood Shop" class, while using a table saw, when the board he was entering into the saw path hit a knot in the board and jerked his hand forward violently, unexpectedly, and rapidly, at which point he realized that he had lost part of his finger. We all realize that having all ten fingers is an advantage when playing basketball. Nevertheless, this son continued to be a fantastic basketball player. However, he did have to undergo, after his initial hand surgery, two more operations to graft new skin onto the end of the still-growing (in length) bone of his finger due to his finger which kept growing through and perforating the skin covering the tip of his partially amputated finger!

Jane's oldest son was a responsible, reverent and Godly son and man! He graduated from high school, entered Junior College played on the Junior College football team, kicked a 64-yard field goal, entered the construction business of building many houses, married Miss California, and raised three daughters as a responsible and Godly man and fantastic father!

Jane's two daughters graduated from high school, and then shortly thereafter were married, each having three children of their own. The youngest daughter pursued a career in cosmetology (haircuts, hair styling, and beauty care), and her older sister became a stay-at-home mother and homemaker.

Jane's younger sister, Ruth, the second member of "Two Sisters, The Dynamic Duo, Pilgrimage to Eternity," was just as amazing and impressive as Jane and truly an inspiration to her family! Ruth, as previously mentioned, was an incredible Big Band and Orchestra dancing partner with her twin brother, Judas. Both Ruth and Judas were blonde children and young adults, during their younger days dancing career, and just happened to be a gorgeous couple, whom most judges may or may not have fully understood or realized that they were actually fraternal twins and siblings with the unfair advantage of having a six-year older sister who was a dance instructor at the University of Southern California (USC) as their personal and private dance tutor or instructor, which was quite serendipitous and advantageous for these beautiful and delightful grammar school and high school dancing twins!

Ruth and her twin, Judas, were also physically fit and accomplished young athletes in grammar school and high school, each participating and excelling in their respective female and male sports teams. Ruth played field hockey and basketball, and her male twin played multiple sports, including basketball and track, amongst others. This physical exercise and sports participation developed tremendously gifted minds and bodies in these two twins, which were of great benefit to them for the remainder of their lives. Ruth was a flautist (flute player), and Judas was a trombonist (slide trombone player) in the high school concert band and marching band, other grammar school and high school activities, which we now know immensely enhances the development of the brains of young children and young adults in a way that no other activity does, with the exceptions of aerobic exercise, powerlifting, and power lifting circuit training in the gym, which all result in superman and wonder woman bodies and brains in males and females, respectively.

What made Ruth a truly deserving recipient of the shared co-title of "Two Sisters, The Dynamic Duo, Pilgrimage to Eternity," along with her older and wise sister, was the very fact that Ruth was a wise, intelligent, reverent, God-fearing, and God-respecting woman of tremendous faith, listening skills, immeasurable humility, discernment, and good judgment. One might even say, without exaggeration, that both Jane and Ruth, also known as "Two Sisters, The Dynamic Duo, Pilgrimage to Eternity," were the ideal, perfect, strongest, most courageous, most powerful or potent, and most enlightened and influential mentors of not only their families, work sites, church communities, and local town colleagues, but also of this entire world! I fully realized this is quite a dramatic statement to make, but see if you agree with me after reading brief descriptions of who these two women actually were, how they cared for others with maximum kindness, generosity, wisdom, caring perspective, attitude and actions, compassion, empathy, grace, mercy, understanding, and how they reacted and responded to adversity, disappointments, frustrating occurrences and events, betrayal by their closest relatives and family members and responded only with kindness, perseverance, and compassion for those who were traitors or evil in their actions or behavior toward and against them.

Jane experienced a true "mid-life crisis" (though not of her own, but rather the result of her husband's unwise and disrespectful behavior toward his wife, Jane), while all her four young children were in grammar school and high school. Her husband had a short affair with another woman and, when discovered and verified by Jane's oldest son, this son, along with Jane, was so upset and disappointed with his father's ungodly behavior and actions that the son punched a hole through the drywall of a room in their house and sustained a transient and minor hand injury, which added potent salt to the original sin and wound created by Jane's husband, Miles, and jeopardizing the Godly love that had previously blessed this family in innumerable ways. Jane, being the fantastic, Godly, forgiving, compassionate, empathetic woman that she was, showed grace and mercy, much like Jesus Christ's death on the cross after being crucified as an innocent man for the sins in his era, all future eras, and even for Jane's husband, Miles, sins and acts of betrayal waged against his lovely and Godly wife. They never were divorced and continued to raise their children despite this massive "bump in the road," during their adventure through life, down the winding and unpredictable road they were trekking on.

Jane was similarly betrayed and extremely disappointed, many other times, during her life by her closest and direct family members, which she communicated to Ruth's youngest son. Only select examples will be elucidated for positive teaching goals as this is most appropriate and was and always would be the recommendation of Jane, who always sought to learn something positive from every experience in her life, good or bad, in order to earn the distinction and honor of being a most compassionate, resilient, forgiving, and enlightened human being, and the example of what all humans can be, with appropriate effort and actions, as taught by Jesus Christ, The Holy Spirit, and her creator, "God The Father" (of all human beings on planet Earth).

Jane owned a second home and offered to rent this home to her granddaughter (the oldest daughter of Jane's older daughter), at a significantly discounted monthly rent. Jane's oldest daughter and granddaughter agreed to the arrangement, then shortly after moving in, completely stopped paying rent! Talking about a very unethical and frustrating close family member's inappropriate actions and behavior, this incident took the Grand Prize for inappropriate behavior and betrayal of a fellow family member's trust in their fellow family member!

Jane's most Godly, responsible, dependable, and oldest son tragically died unexpectedly of a rare condition at an early age. Although he was married to a former "Miss California" beauty pageant winner, his "Miss California" wife was a "Prima donna" (not at all referring to a chief female singer in an opera or opera company), narcissist, completely selfish, verbally and emotionally abusive, a terrible mother, not a mentor in any sense of the word, and brutally cruel and disparaging to her loving and Godly husband! Just one brief example (not to dwell on the negative but to enlighten others with a positive teaching example of how not to behave in life), and a true story will be offered to and elucidated for all sincere readers who wish to avoid the sinful, inappropriate, selfish, and devastating acts that other "non-mentor" humans dastardly enact to manipulate or take advantage of others instead of caring for other human beings that they interact with daily. These sinful and selfish people do exist in this generation and every generation, unfortunately, and thus, every human should be prepared to recognize them, deal in a strong and godly manner with them, or in certain circumstances altogether avoid or circumvent them, to ensure your serenity and safety, especially if your goals and aspirations include embarking on a pilgrimage to eternity to be reunited with God your creator, after the conclusion of your physical body's life on this Earth. In the paragraphs below, Ruth's youngest son will share with the reader the genuinely evil and ungrateful behavior and actions of "Prima donna Miss California," the wife from hell.

When Jane's eldest son died prematurely and unexpectedly from a rare medical condition and diagnosis, the eldest son's wife took the most expensive car among her husband's classic collectible cars and then gave all the other cars of her husband to her husband's younger sisters, then, in cahoots with her husband's younger siblings, informed Jane that she would not pay a penny (the smallest amount of money in the United States dollar currency), for her husband's funeral and memorial service, to be held at the local Christian church where her husband had, for many years and at the time of his unexpected and sudden death, been employed by the church in an important leadership role.

When Jane asked her remaining children to contribute, again a frustration of Jane personally communicated to the author, financially to the expenses of their oldest brother and sibling, the remaining living children were unexpectedly unwilling and noncooperative. Jane, on her own, ended up fully financing all the expenses of her beloved oldest son's funeral and memorial service, without any support or financial contributions from her oldest son's sinister, selfish, and narcissistic wife, and sadly, from all her oldest son's siblings. Jane faithfully and generously organized and orchestrated a truly magnificent funeral and memorial service at her son's Christian church and site of employment (for numerous years before his untimely death). Kudos to Godly, dynamic Jane for being the definition of "Best Mother Ever" despite abandonment of her eldest son by her son's Prima donna, selfish, evil wife, and her co-conspirators, to heap the entire financial obligation and burden of completing her dear son's funeral, which he was so worthy of and deserved as a result of his being, his whole life, an exceptional, outstanding, responsible, Godly son, father, and sibling who was very supportive at all times to and for his parents, brothers, and sisters throughout the entirety of these family members' lives, despite their lack of reciprocal respect, behavior, and actions.

Jane was later put in an assisted living facility by her two daughters and rarely visited by her children near the end of her life. Ruth's youngest son frequently visited Jane near the end of her life in this assisted living facility and was delighted to know and experience firsthand that she was the same, along with her younger sister Ruth, "Two Sisters, The Dynamic Duo, Pilgrimage To Eternity," Godly, forgiving, compassionate, merciful, gracious, kind, and loving woman that Ruth's youngest son had always known and loved like a second mother, up until the day of her physical body death on Earth and simultaneous spiritual and physical transition into and onto her path and pilgrimage to eternity, where she continues her spiritual life journey with God, who "so-blessed" and created her with the most loving and Godly traits, characteristics, and behaviors that this planet has ever known.

Ruth, Jane's youngest sister, was a prominent, significant, and most influential, aside from God, blessing to and best friend of Jane her entire life. Ruth, the most faithful, kind, loving, and dependable sibling to Jane, also immensely benefitted from the loving, kind, caring, optimal mentor "that was her elder and wise sister," Jane.

Unfortunately, both Jane and Ruth experienced nearly identical circumstances and unexpected, disappointing behavior and acts of betrayal by both their husbands.

We will leave it at that for now. Ruth was a kind, Godly, forgiving, compassionate, full of grace and mercy child, teenager, university student, career woman (occupational therapist), and wife. Ruth's youngest son did not learn the magnificent, almost untold, and benevolent, fantastic history and full story about his mother's entire loving and kind life, sadly or happily, depending on your positive or negative life perspective, until he met all his mother's grammar school, high school, university, and other dearest friends and acquaintances, on the day of his mother's funeral and memorial service at the gravesite, his mother's wish, in the same cemetery where Ruth's loving parents were both buried and where her older sister and her older sister's husband (Jane was forever forgiving on this Earth and quite certainly continues to display and bestow on others this characteristic and trait in heaven for eternity) were both buried, in Claremont, New Hampshire.

During Ruth's university education in California, she joined, though raised as a Methodist denomination Christian and not brought up as a Mormon, a Mormon Sorority House. God, in some unknown manner allowed and promoted this occurrence and enabled Ruth to gradually adjust to the more diverse cultural population of students that were present at and attending San Jose State University than she had experienced and grown up within Claremont, New Hampshire. This was indeed God's enlightening gift to Ruth throughout her university educational experience. Ruth was able to learn from and make friends with university students from myriad countries and diverse cultural and religious upbringings and backgrounds and develop harmonious, authentic, genuine, and sincere friendships with all these university students while living in Delta Zeta Sorority House, where alcohol, drug abuse, and sexual relations were prohibited, a further fantastic gift to Ruth from God, allowing her to focus on her undergraduate university studies to pursue and successfully complete and achieve her dream of being an occupational therapist whilst also forming friendships and making friends from throughout the world and of various fascinating backgrounds, cultures, countries, and other religions, which were of great benefit to her Godly world perspective, compassion, and empathy toward all people of all skin colors and cultures throughout the world, and for the duration of her entire future career. Ruth lived a God-blessed, caring, and altruistic life.

At Ruth's funeral, her youngest son who organized and singly financed the funeral and memorial services, had the greatest pleasure and honor of his life, in his opinion, in hearing the stories of his mother, Ruth, firsthand and directly from all the individuals, some who had known her for eighty years! All the grammar school, high school, university, and all other friends who graciously attended Ruth's funeral, eighty years after her birth, and most of whom also attended and participated in a "lunch gathering, celebration of an Angelic life, and remembrances session" regarding the highlights and blessings of Ruth's existence on Earth that were experienced firsthand and forever remembered and relished by all her closest friends and classmates from her birth until her death 80 years later, at an old, antique, and classic "train car diner restaurant" in downtown Claremont, New Hampshire, following the burial ceremony and memorial service led by the Methodist church pastor and Ruth's youngest son, both of whom had nothing but positive praise, admiration, and respect for the person Ruth had been, always was, and always will be, in her life journey, along with her older sister, now reunited forever, as they both hoped and wished for in "Two Sisters, The Dynamic Duo, Pilgrimage to Eternity," their dual and concomitant life stories, now realized, at least concerning their amazing physical body, mind, and spiritual lives on this Earth, and the realization and commencement of their new and joyful beginning of their recreated, extraordinary, upgraded, and optimized physical body, mind, and spiritual lives, united as two loving sisters as they have always known, in their pilgrimage into eternity alongside their Creator and The Holy Trinity: Jesus Christ, The Holy Spirit, and God The Father.

Just a few revelations and elucidations learned by Ruth's youngest son, by God's grace, on the day of his mother's funeral service that he would have otherwise never known due to the fact that his mother was too meek, humble, and modest to ever brag about herself or her extraordinary life to either of her two fantastic and grateful sons, who revere their "God's best gift to them, their mother," now and up until the day of their physical body deaths, and thereafter, during their own pilgrimages to Eternity, with God their mother demonstrated to them through her loving, kind, Godly behavior, and by taking both her sons to church with her throughout their lives while growing up with her in grammar school and high school, every Sunday, and ensuring that both her boys respected God and lived their lives as close as possible to how Jesus Christ, God's son and the "best-ever" example of how humans on Earth can and should live their lives in a Godly manner while simultaneously following and respecting God's intentions and actions to guide and protect his creations, lived his life on Earth as God's gift to humans and redeemer of all human's sins, such that all humans can be forgiven of their shortcomings and sins, and be reunited in heaven with God upon their physical body death on Earth, at which time all humans may, by their faith in Jesus Christ, then begin their spiritual pilgrimage to eternity to live with their God forever. (Many might call this a run-on sentence, but Ruth's youngest son believes this sentence is one priceless, all-inclusive, and vitally importance message of continuity and a fully integrated concept that must not be "broken into multiple puzzle pieces" merely to pacify the "proper English grammar obsessive compulsives!")

Revelation One, learned by Ruth's sons at her funeral by her friends and personal historians and biographers, was that Ruth was truly loved, admired, and immeasurably respected by all her classmates, due to her non-intrusive nature, kindness, humility, meekness, captivating and spellbinding smile, positive attitude, supreme listening skills, and unmatched beauty throughout her life, truly rare and scarce but not an impossible compilation of concomitant attributes for a human being, as demonstrated by Ruth during her entire life! Ruth's youngest son waited, unknowingly, fifty-five years to learn that his mother was voted "Prom Queen" by her senior year classmates in both high school and university! He not only saw pictures in high school and college yearbooks as proof of these facts, but he also was afforded the unmatched and priceless gift of reading actual inscriptions from yearbooks owned by Ruth from high school and college and her many classmates, who were all very admiring and showed tremendous love and respect for Ruth in the comments that were made both for and to Ruth and by Ruth for and to her fellow admired, loved, and respected classmates! All the males who attended Ruth's funeral stated that they all have loved (conceptually, not physically!), admired, and respected Ruth so much while in school with her and were all saddened, yet happy for her when she left New Hampshire to commence her university undergraduate education in California, and then again when they received news that she had married a California man she met while they were both in college. Ruth's son also had the privilege and honor of joining Ruth and her elder sister, Jane, when they attended 40 and 45-year Stevens High School reunion dinners and parade events in Claremont, New Hampshire, where other new revelations were learned by Ruth's son, such as the fact, as told by the Center (tallest basketball player on the team), and basketball team teammate of Ruth who played alongside Ruth on the female high school basketball team, stated that Ruth was an outstanding fast, relentless, energetic runner, rebounder, and point-shooting guard on their Stevens High School women's basketball team, whom that Center teammate could never forget due to her dynamic performance every basketball game that she played in grammar school and high school!

Another revelation to Ruth's two sons was a coworker occupational therapist who had worked with their mother for over twenty years, who visited Ruth's house after having taken another job in a different California city, who made an unforgettable statement about Ruth. He stated:

"Your mother was the most Godly, respectable, and the best listener I have ever met. She was also the most kind, compassionate, empathetic, and positive occupational therapist coworker I ever had the pleasure and opportunity to work with. I hope you appreciate and respect her as much as I forever will, and that your life will be as blessed as possible as a result of the amazing person she is and tries to be every day in every aspect of her Godly and kind life!"

CHAPTER SEVEN

Unexpected, Exciting, Entertaining Dating Experiences And Life-Long Friends Made During Their Experiences, Ultimately Leading To The Marriages Of Both Dynamic Duo Sisters.

Jane and Ruth, the oldest sister and youngest sister, were both the daughters of Alex and Sharon from Claremont, New Hampshire, and both had excellent experiences during their undergraduate university studies. Both Jane and Ruth dated attractive and intelligent men and made many friends from various countries and cultures worldwide. Ruth dated and was very attracted to a Japanese man and university premedical student in one instance. She loved this man very much and thought fondly of this man throughout her life. She ultimately married another man. This "other man" was a first-year University of California Berkeley student.

God has a plan for everyone's life, and who are we to question God's plan for our life? What many "armchair historians" might prematurely or, in a prejudiced way, decide is a mistake by God when they review the history of adverse events in a person's life and decide that they should not have had certain relationships with specific individuals, God can easily refute because of God's omniscience, omnipresence, and omnipotence. God, being outside humans' time zone with regard to the past, present, and future, can see all three (past, present, and future) simultaneously and knows all the learning, growth, resilience, compassion, blessings, and enlightenment that all humans are capable of attaining by navigating through the world, with God's presence, protection, and guidance.

In Ruth's specific situation, she married the man she chose and loved, had two amazing boys, and taught them all she knew (a tremendous amount), which gifted and empowered them with genius-like attributes, abilities, and achievements throughout their lives. Ruth was the zenith, optimal mentor to her two boys throughout their lives, and was recognized by both her sons and God as a most remarkable and Godly woman, perhaps one of the most outstanding motherly mentors who has ever lived on

Earth, and whom will exist spiritually and physically (upgraded and with zenith optimization) with God in heaven for eternity!

In Jane's specific situation, she married the Pepperdine University star basketball student whom she loved, had two amazing boys and two girls and taught them all she knew (a tremendous amount), was the zenith, optimal mentor to her two boys and two girls throughout their and her life, and was recognized by both her sons, both her daughters (although questionable at times due to their naive and poor judgment), and God as one of the most incredible women and Godly mentors who has ever lived and served God's purposes and intentions while on Earth and whilst performing their Godly and Angelic mentor roles to all other humans on Earth during their remarkable and spellbinding lives.

Jane, the oldest daughter of Alex and Sharon, during the completion of her undergraduate university premedical courses at the University of Southern California (USC), met, dated, and eventually married the one man love of her life, which she remained married to for the duration of her life, and was eventually and ultimately buried with, after her husband Sam's earlier death from a specified medical condition, and shared a tombstone inscription with, which was prominently displayed over their grave site plot. Jane, like all Godly, forgiving, "one-spouse-committed-females (Angels)," vowed during her wedding to love (and forgive) her spouse until their death, which she honored, again as expected from a loving, faithful, committed, Godly spouse and wife to her beloved (but far from perfect) husband.

Ruth, the youngest daughter of Alex and Sharon, during the completion of her undergraduate university occupational therapy degree courses at San Jose State University in California, met, dated, and eventually married the one man love of her life, which she remained faithful to and married to for the duration of her life, until her husband abandoned her, had multiple affairs with other women while still married to Ruth, and eventually (and in an evil manner) sent her divorce-related documents, sent deliberately on Ruth's marriage anniversary date or on Valentine's Day, to add insult to injury. Ruth, like all Godly, forgiving, one-spouse-committed-females (or Angels)," vowed during her wedding to love (and forgive) her spouse until their death, which she honored, again as expected from a loving, faithful, committed, Godly spouse and Angelic wife to her beloved (but far from perfect), husband.

Nobody gets through this life without frustration, disappointing people or events in their life, sinful or evil acts directed at them, or perpetrated against them, and opportunities to forgive other people of one or more dastardly and dark or malicious intent or action. Above are just several examples of situations where "Two Sisters, The Dynamic Duo, Pilgrimage To Eternity" was experienced, adverse events were overcome, and both sisters were stronger, having navigated through their own personal stormy oceans and journeys with God as their "mariner's astrolabe," "back staff," "octant," "sextant," "magnetic compass," or "global positioning satellite (GPS) systems, range and depth finders, and map measurers."

CHAPTER EIGHT

Early Occupation And Family Days Of Dynamic Duo Sisters, Two Boys And Two Girls for (Elder) Sister One And Two Boys For (Younger) Sister Two, And Struggles To Balance Work Life and Family/Parenting Duties And Responsibilities

Jane, shortly after her university education at USC (the University of Southern California), married Sam and commenced having (giving birth to) her family of four children. Her four children consisted of Tim, the oldest son; then Lisa, the oldest daughter; then Lena, the youngest daughter; and finally, Jacob, the youngest son. These four children were given as a blessing from God to Jane and her husband Sam over a period of ten years. All the mothers of four or more children know and can verify that this is like having four simultaneous, full-time jobs at once, then pretending every day that you have time to have a beautiful, calm, serene, peaceful life of your own, all such a lovely dream (and fantasy) indeed! Her husband went to work each workday and many weekends to his role and occupation of being the superintendent of his children's future junior high school. He also worked as a security guard at Disneyland in Orange County, CA, on various weekdays, weeknights, and weekends. You can only imagine how busy yet capable Jane was daily, raising her four children each day while her husband was diligently working at one or both jobs each week, providing financial support for his wife and children.

Ruth, living approximately six hours away from her elder sister in California, upon graduation from San Jose State University, also was married and had two sons, who were approximately two years different in age. Her husband initially, in the earliest years of their marriage, started a Master's Degree program, while Ruth was diligently working as an occupational therapist and raising her two sons. Her husband was teaching at the local high school in town. Despite spending many hours away from home during her husband's Master's degree program endeavor, her husband failed to follow through and complete the program, a considerable disappointment to both Ruth and her husband during a hectic time in both their lives and the lives of their two children. Ruth's husband, Jerry, was consistent in embarking on vacations each summer because, as a high school teacher, he would have at least two months off (or three if he did not sign up to teach students during 1-month summer school sessions), to plan and execute outdoor travel trips by car or backpacking up different mountains or through mountain ranges, or being involved in his two boys' summer sports leagues, e.g., baseball, swimming, tennis, and others.

Both Sam and Jerry, the husbands of the "Two Sisters, The Dynamic Duo, Pilgrimage to Eternity" book and future movie cast stars, had an uncanny similarity in their tendency toward (and carried out treachery actions of), promiscuity in the latter half of their married lives, an extremely stressful and tortuous trial of resiliency and inner strength for both sisters, Jane and Ruth, and their six total children, had great expectations that their spouses would be the ultimate, zenith morality and ethics mentors and demonstrators to both them (and all six children), whom they had pledged and vowed to honor and respect as their wives until their death during both Sam and Jerry's distinct weddings and the wedding vows portion of their wedding ceremonies.

Sam had an affair for several years that was eventually discovered by Sam and Jane's eldest son, who was so upset that (Sam was lucky he was not the wall in the home that day), the oldest son punched a hole in the wall of his house the day he learned that his father was having an affair with another woman who was not his dear, kind, loving, and Godly mother, Jane. This event nearly disintegrated the family bonds of the entire household and almost, except by God and Jane's grace and mercy, resulted in a divorce that would have devastated or severely impacted the love of all the children for their parents. Luckily, Jane was the bigger and stronger of the two parents, and graciously, compassionately, mercifully "let it go" and forgave her husband, Sam, for his egregious sins and acts of treachery. God bless Jane and her spiritual power and strength, gifts from God, that enabled her to endure these troubling times until she and her husband were able to "work things out" by "forgiving and (attempting to) forgetting" these negative events, and trials and tribulations created unnecessarily and cruelly by her husband Sam. Sam, in all fairness, was a better or "improved" husband after this catastrophe, and actually thereafter remained faithful to his deserving wife until his death many years later, after both Jane and Sam navigated many other storms in their life, involving their children and grandchildren, who had many of their own shocking problem and travesties and unimaginable life paths, eventually, luckily, and finally arriving as less chaotic life destinations as more mature and "learned the hard way" adults.

Jerry (aka Jerry Lee), as a high school teacher, struggled to maintain command and leadership during his high school class teaching sessions. For whatever reasons, he found this task difficult or near-impossible and received regular evaluations that said as much or more than had been stated and divulged in these paragraphs. He also was reprimanded for inappropriate comments to various, presumably, gorgeous high school female students in his classes, on multiple occasions, much to the chagrin of his wife and two sons. His two sons did not "find out" these depressing and disappointing facts until after their father retired, and again, in great detail by reading actual administrative teacher evaluations regarding their father, just after Ruth's death, luckily and by God's and Ruth's grace and mercy, as a result of Ruth's hiding these shocking revelations about their teacher and father in safe and locked files that were not discovered until after Ruth's death when her two boys were cleaning up Ruth's loving home.

Ruth had to be exceptionally merciful and strong to not share her frustrations and disappointments, on many occasions from the reports reviewed, with her two loving sons who would definitely have comforted her and shown great sympathy, empathy, and compassion for her during every episode of disappointment if they had only known about this egregious behavior of their father. At the same time, both boys (Ruth's two sons) understood why their mother hid these events and written reports of these occurrences (committed by their father) from both her sons, namely, to prevent them from disrespecting or even hating their father for his unethical and inappropriate attitudes, perspectives, repeated acts of indiscretion, and malevolent actions and behavior. Ruth was the best Angel that "Jerry Lee" could ever have been given by God to protect him from his own evil aspirations, attitudes, and actions (if he had recognized and embraced the Angel God sent him, which he ignored and disrespected throughout his life and the life of the Angel sent to him from God), such that his children could respect and obey him while they were growing up and developing into the magnificent children and adults they became, despite their father's less-than-optimal mentor behavior and actions, and largely due to or majority credit due to their Angelic and Godly (the second of the "Two Sisters,

The Dynamic Duo, Pilgrimage to Eternity"), mother who was the greatest listener of all time, and after her death, earning the title of the greatest hider of negative father information and poor teacher behavior evaluations of all time as well! God bless Ruth for the Angel she was not only to her somewhat misguided or even sinister spouse and husband (in retrospect, thank God), but more importantly, to her beloved and blessed (by their mother and God) children, which she shielded and protected, wisely and benevolently, from unnecessary news that would have jolted both sons and likely resulted in their partial or total loss of respect and admiration for their father while they were in grammar school and high school, and before or during their university undergraduate and graduate school education en route to receiving a doctorate degree!

"Jerry Lee," Ruth's husband, would later further disappoint, frustrate, and attempt to (debatable whether he was successful, as sinister as he turned out to be), crush the heart, soul, and love of his wife for him, despite all his despicable perspectives, attitudes, and underhanded actions of disrespect for her. When "Jerry Lee" experienced the eventual death of his father, step-father, and mother, he, despite knowing that his wife, Ruth, knew she was in the "will" of his parents, along with both Ruth's sons, also listed in the "will" to receive divulged (at least to the two boy's mother) amounts of money from Jerry's parents (or paternal grandparents, in the case of the two sons of Jerry and Ruth), upon their death and execution of the "will" that was predetermined and explained by Jerry's parents to both Jerry and Ruth. Despite these facts, when Jerry's parents both died, Jerry dishonored his parents by ignoring their "will (inheritance intentions and godly goals)" and stealing all the inheritance for his selfish and sinister self (a truly Satanic and unGodly act). Most people would say this is quite a disappointment. They would be correct!

Jerry later added to his resume of being a despicable, unloving husband by separating from his wife, having sexual encounters, and affairs, dating or living with approximately six different females, all while he was still legally married to his loving and Godly wife, whom he had disrespected, neglected, and repeatedly hurt in many ways throughout their married life. Luckily, both sons of Jerry and Ruth were out of the house away at university when all these acts of marriage and wife betrayal were committed by the winner of "most irresponsible and unloving husband, despite being blessed with an Angelic wife, which he never deserved but was blessed by God just the same, with her entry into his otherwise misguided, misdirected, and chaotic life of disappointments, giving him two sons as blessings from God despite his sinful nature," award. One can only imagine or surmise how such a man could marry a woman who was so "out of his league." God has compassion on all his creations, despite any preexisting evil or sinister nature and inclinations, as evidenced by "Jerry Lee" being bestowed with an Angel from God. Unfortunately, Jerry failed to respect and nurture God's gift to him, and one day, he will face God and the consequences for not only one but all of his ungodly perspectives, attitudes, aspirations, and misbehavior and transgressions. Good luck to Jerry, perhaps God's mercy will be bestowed on you despite your sins and betrayal for no one was more kind and merciful than the Angel sent from God to you, Jerry, yet do not assume nor be so naive as to imagine there will not be negative, harmful, and adverse consequences for your ungodly behavior and acts of betrayal regarding your loving, Godly, and angelic wife…time (or lack of access to eternity with God) will tell!

CHAPTER NINE

Truly Angelic Compassion, Empathy, Generosity, Humility, Morality, Ethical Behavior, Shunning of Alcohol Or Drug Abuse, Demonstration Of Unparalleled Listening Skills, Altruistic And Motherly Supportive Behavior, And A+ Mother Ratings For These Dynamic Duo Sisters

Jane's husband, Miles, drank alcohol in moderation and was a coffee-drinking addict. He was not a smoker, thankfully, and thus a good non-smoking role model and mentor for his observant four children.

Unfortunately for his children, his drinking of alcohol, even though in moderation was a devastating observation for two of his four children, who later became raging and aggressive alcoholics, his youngest daughter suffering from alcohol dependence and tobacco dependence, and his youngest son suffering from alcohol dependence and multiple years of substance abuse, and multiple marriages were destroyed simultaneously and consecutively for both siblings. Being a good mentor by not drinking alcohol was not in the cards dealt to Jane's husband, Miles.

Who was the greatest mentor and role model for Jane's four children growing up? Of course, the answer is Jane herself. Despite her busy life raising four children, almost alone all day and every day, due to her husband working days and nights and weekends outside the house and at distant work sites, Jane did manage to find leadership positions in various charitable organizations and even became a board member of Disneyland, the famous amusement park for young, innocent, impressionable children and adults alike that, in the past, promoted American Christian family values and attitudes, which have made America stand out as a great country due to these Godly and life-enhancing teachings and values (at least in the past, before it became "woke" and started promoting non-Christian values and promoting homosexual and transgender perspectives and attitudes, and even tailored their marketing and advertising to not only attract these individuals to their theme parks but also to promote their deviant and ungodly lifestyles in their Disney movies, toys, and movie and toy characters, which has been an insult and extraordinary act of disrespect to traditional American Founding Fathers Christian American values and intent for the United States of America).

Jane was a tremendous, loving, active listener and Godly mentor to all four of her children throughout their upbringing and also to her younger sister and two nephews. Jane would take all six children to Disneyland and Knott's Berry Farm and all the beaches in Orange County and San Diego County, California, SeaWorld, and the San Diego Zoo. Jane and Ruth were always excellent and organized planners whose preparation for fantastic family "get-togethers" were unparalleled and resulted in truly joyful events and gatherings of love, without exception (a feat not easily accomplished in some families), during holidays and non-holiday family events throughout the United States of America.

Neither Jane nor Ruth chose to drink alcohol or abuse drugs or become excessive coffee addicts. This may seem like an insignificant observation or statement but is a critically important aspect, feature, and characteristic of all outstanding role models and mentors in life for not only young children but also young and older adults, as this will extend their lives, brain health, and physical health and development. God bless the "Two Sisters, The Dynamic Duo, Pilgrimage to Eternity" and their demonstration of a Godly path through this life on Earth and a successful pilgrimage to eternity, by living the life God, their creator, prescribed and intended for them, taking the "good times" and "bad times" in stride, not overreacting in rage or viciousness, but instead looking long-term into the future and attempting always, with God's strength, support, guidance, grace, and mercy to make the best decision for their families, despite being abused either physically or mentally or disrespectfully by either their children or husbands/spouses, and always seeking and embracing the positive aspect in every difficult and problematic situation and transforming (e.g., caterpillars into beautiful Monarch butterflies) these situations and occurrences into learning experiences. They employed and masterfully executed this protocol during and throughout each and every travesty in their lives, thereby protecting their children from unnecessary and extremely negative circumstances that might impede their learning, loving, and Godly development as children, teenagers, young adults, and seasoned older adults (all age group categories otherwise known as "children of God," regardless of age category, in God's eyes)!

Jane, many years after the birth of her four lovely children, would later, along with her younger sister Ruth and Ruth's youngest son, come to the rescue of her two youngest children, who, by themselves, were on a misguided and down-spiraling path to hell and death from alcohol and substance abuse, literally on the edge of death in both cases, both children (now adults with many years of alcohol and substance abuse, brain, body (liver), social, spiritual death and destructive damage already done and near death, figuratively and literally), had suffered many years of decline, both having lost their spouses to divorce due to their selfish and addiction priorities of alcohol and substance abuse, before priorities such as love, support, and protection (e.g., not driving the children to school and other activities while completely inebriated, e.g., drunk, and apt to kill their family member in a drunk driving accident), of their spouse and young children. Both Jane's youngest children, now adults, were concomitantly being the worst possible parents and mentors for their children by demonstrating no leadership and letting their addictions take precedence over their love, mentoring, support, and Godly guidance of their children regarding how to behave during their childhood, teenager, and adult lives.

Eventually and after years of trying to help both these youngest children and, now adults, yet still behaving like children, Jane, Ruth, and Ruth's youngest son were successful in lovingly persuading and convincing these individuals to enter outpatient, then necessary and vitally important and required, essential inpatient alcohol and substance dependency rehabilitation programs. Relapses occurred in both, and two rehabilitation programs were necessary for Lena, and three rehabilitation programs were required for Jacob.

These programs saved their lives. Jacob eventually, when sober, married a third time and has been happily married and sober ever since. Lena chose not to remarry but has returned to her status of being a loving and caring mother, with great success, luckily for both her and her three loving and devoted children.

One can only imagine (and dread, like a horror movie) what would have happened to Lena and Jacob, and their spouses and children, had Jane, Ruth, and Ruth's son not intervened successfully and persuaded both these individuals that death would have preceded any other event in their lives, had they not entered rehabilitation (this was the truth, by the way) exactly when they did.

Ironically and sadly, these individuals, even after completing rehabilitation, have not fully embraced the grace and mercy God provided them in the times of their desperation and great need, and they also have neglected, intentionally or unintentionally, to fully thank, embrace, and forever love and respect what the three individuals listed above did for them in their time of greatest need.

Luckily again, and by God's grace and blessings, these three, e.g., "Two Sisters, The Dynamic Due" and Ruth's son, neither required nor ever demanded thanks because they were already blessed and full of love, provided to them by their God and creator, Jesus Christ, The Holy Spirit, and God The Father, also known as The Holy Trinity!

Both Lena and Jacob are alive and thriving today, enjoying the observation of their "family tree" growth, as evidenced by their children and grandchildren, all the result of God's grace and mercy in their lives.

Despite Not Receiving The Deserved And Expected Support And Love From Their Spouses, Family Members, And Colleagues, Both Dynamic Duo Sisters Excelled In Every Category Of Their Lives, Engendered The Greatest Love, Appreciation, And Respect From All Their Children, Despite Their Human Imperfections, That Could Ever Be Envisioned or Imagined And Were The Greatest Angelic Role Model Mothers

That Their Children Could Have Ever Hoped
For Or Imagined Possible

Jane and Ruth never had excess money to spoil and splurge on and for their children or their spouses. They raised their children, one by one, as they were born and developing into young adults and were forced, thankfully, by God and a low-level financial budget each month to replace extravagant spending on their children with focused and wise, healthy food purchases and motherly and angelic love and support which they provided to all their children twenty-four hours per day. Precocious and eager to learn new and enlightening, health-protecting and Godly Holy Spirit-provided knowledge, and blessed with godly wisdom and outstanding university educations, these "Two Sisters, The Dynamic Duo, Pilgrimage to Eternity," costarred in roles that they had embarked on from their birth up until the day of their physical deaths, achieving unmatched wisdom, love, kindness, and Godly qualities during their fantastic journey involving the raising of their children, guiding their children to be responsible Godly adults, always displaying and demonstrating good manners, as ideal mentors of their children, never expecting too much or forcing them to be someone they were not willing to be or interested in being, yet from birth, reassuring them that they (their children) had unlimited potential to achieve remarkable and benevolent accomplishments in life, and through honest, ethical, and moral behavior, preparation, training, and work, they could achieve spellbinding dreams they had (and even dreams they had never imagined), both for themselves and for others in their lives. By achieving these successful accomplishments, even without the expected help from their less-than-perfect spouses and always smiling, being a source of happiness for all those around them, and "keeping their eyes on the prize" of God's salvation and redemption of their physical bodies and souls upon their days of demise, they both then victoriously transitioned from their lives on this Earth to their pilgrimage to eternity with God in heaven. They are truly remarkable women in every sense!

Jane became a volunteer board member of many organization throughout Orange County, California, that sought to help the less fortunate humans in our word, children, abused spouses, impoverished, homeless, or substance abuse and alcohol dependent and addicted individuals alike. Though she was never paid for her roles in these organizations, and ironically, criticized by her husband and children for these roles and acts of kindness and Godliness, she persevered and continued to be a vital and proactive fund-raising Angelic figure for all these organizations, who were and will be forever indebted (not financially, but spiritually), to her for her genuinely altruistic work, accomplished over the many years of her dynamic and life-changing, self-less contributions to society and the world.

Ruth was blessed to have received a position through her daily employment, as a professional occupational therapist, helping those with or without mental illness, who had strokes, accidents, or other injuries or surgeries, which required the professional knowledge and expertise of occupational therapists, to re-learn or practice until the perfection of the previous coordinated physical actions and movements were restored to their pre-stroke, pre-accident, pre-injury, or pre-surgery level of function. You can only imagine the great satisfaction an occupational therapist derives and appreciates after seeing their clients or patients, day-by-day, slowly or rapidly resume their ability to function physically, spiritually, emotionally, and socially after major adverse events or unexpected setbacks that positioned them in these situations requiring the loving care and assistance that physical therapists and occupational therapists professionally provide to their patients on a daily basis, often without any positive feedback from their patients, yet gratefully and graciously appreciated when received.

In Ruth's later years, she required the love and support of her twin brother, younger brother, and youngest son (her oldest son was willing, but not available to help in this specific situation), to clean up and organize her home and finances, then move her to a more kind, supportive, and interactive community so that she could be healthier (physically, mentally/emotionally, socially, and spiritually) with similar-age community members to ensure that her overall health would be maintained and supported or even enhanced by a proactive move to a fresh community. At the necessary and essential (for Ruth) request by Ruth's youngest son, a meeting was arranged between Ruth's son, Ruth's twin brother, and Ruth's youngest brother to organize and schedule an intervention to help, assist, and proactively demonstrate support, assistance, love, and affection for the future health and well-being of Ruth into her senior wisdom phase of life.

The plan consisted of arriving at Ruth's hometown, all three helpers living out of town, on Friday evening, discussing Ruth's home cleaning and move to a more healthy and supportive environment and community with senior citizens that she could communicate and interact with daily to socialize and maintain her happiness and fulfillment in communicating and sharing her life experiences and accomplishments with others of her generation and even participate in senior dance, art, concerts, field trips that were entertaining and life-fulfilling among her generational friends, colleagues, and local community members, an altruistic goal and endeavor for this group gathering to preserve and, hopefully, enhance the present and future health of Ruth. The plan was to arrive Friday evening, clean up the home on Saturday, Sunday, Monday, and Tuesday, after which Ruth's son had to depart to a required professional conference out of town and out of state, which commenced on Wednesday. Ruth's son was scheduled for a desired professional conference and professional skill certification course on Saturday which he reluctantly canceled as a sacrifice to help and assist his mother, along with his two uncles, who agreed to this plan to help and assist their loving sister.

Treachery and the two brothers' abuse of their sister then exploded into catastrophe! Ruth's son drove six hours to his mother's home town, rented a room at a local motel for five days, and awaited the expected Friday evening arrival, as discussed, planned, and as was agreed upon by his two uncles, the "brothers" of Ruth. Ruth's son missed his professional certification course (for a novel procedure and technique) he had planned on attending and completing the next day, Saturday, as a sacrifice of love and affection for his mother, who was most precious, admired, and loved for her many acts of Angelic nature and intent, throughout his upbringing, education, and maturation from a child to a doctorate-level educated professional whose life was dedicated to helping others have a better life every day he worked until his death. Despite the sacrifices, Ruth's son made to ensure the success of this trip and mission to help his mother, his uncles were arrogantly and blasphemously selfish, evil, and disrespectful to not only the entire mission and plan to help their sister, but also betrayed and deceptively created a scapegoat and "make-believe enemy" of their sister, namely, their sister's son, who was falsely described by Ruth's "dastardly duo brothers" as "someone who neither cared for her or loved her, and who had abandoned her," all devised as a sinister plot to cover-up for both uncles' sinful behavior of deciding last minute to attend a "Berkeley and Stanford football game" instead of helping their sister as planned, and both uncles arrived three days later than scheduled, thus delaying and destroying the plan to help clean up their sister's home and arrange her move to a more supportive community and environment to maximize her future health and well-being. Having not arrived, functionally and physically, until Monday, four days after their planned arrival; her two uncles then tried feverishly to justify their sinful and evil neglect of their sister's needs for their support and assistance, to their sister's son, who had canceled his professional certification course on Saturday, and was then stranded in a motel for three days with nothing to do, unable to start this mission without his disappointing and irresponsible, neglectful two uncles who placed their own selfish desires over and above the desperate needs and support that their loving sister required to restore her health and well-being.

Ruth's son and the two uncles, both uncles being despicable in every respect and demonstrating the poorest judgment and irresponsibility in not even apologizing to their sister's son for going to a football game and, as a consequence, blowing up the entire weekend work plan, showing up four days later than planned, then both uncles made matters worse after Ruth's son worked exhaustively for 48 hours with his two uncles on Monday and Tuesday by convincing Ruth on Wednesday, after Ruth's son had to depart for his next pre-paid and required distinct professional education and training conference, which was out of state, that her son "had abandoned her, no longer cared for her, and that she could only trust and depend on them, her brothers (aka, traitors and uncaring, unloving sinister brothers), and brainwashed her into thinking her son had not come to help. These two sinister brothers, the arrogant and atheist youngest brother and the older coward and despicable traitor fraternal twin brother of Ruth, further betrayed, lied to, and brainwashed their sister into thinking that she should stay in her house, which was filled to the ceiling with trash and other debris in every room with no functioning water supply or electricity, and every room in the house had not been cleaned for many years. They deceitfully pacified her and convinced her to stay in her home because they refused to have the courage to do the right thing that had been the original plan for this assistance trip to rescue Ruth from disaster, namely cleaning up the home, moving her out, selling the home and using these funds to transition her to a senior community where she could make friends, socialize, receive assistance in activities of daily living, and maintain her mental and physical health in a community of similar-age friends and colleagues. Both brothers backstabbed their sister, later revealing to Ruth's son that they decided to "leave her in her home until her mind was gone (approximately seven years later), at which time it would be easier to move her to assisted living or memory facility." The two "despicable duo brothers," in a "quick and easy way out" manner, and secondary to their laziness, selfishness, and sinful intent to not do what they both knew their sister needed to have any chance of maintaining her mental and physical health for the next one to two decades, and instead took the easy route in their approach to their" (angelic) sister-in-need," to the detriment of their loving but desperate sister, and decided to abandon their loving and trusting sister (her judgment was obviously impaired, especially concerning the faithfulness of her two "dastardly duo brothers"), who she, unfortunately and incorrectly, thought that she could both trust and depend on that her brothers would be honest, ethical, and moral in helping her clean up her condemned home (the judgment the public health department declared which specifically stated "the home was a public health hazard and not fit to be lived in by anyone, including its owner Ruth, until it is cleaned up and the plumbing repaired, and air conditioning, heating, and water supply are restored and functioning," regarding her home during the days of this trip), and then assist her with making life-improving decisions based on wise judgment, discernment, and love for their angelic and loving sister. Unfortunately, this plan, wish, and dream of Ruth's loving son did not come to fruition.

The original intended goal of Ruth's son, when he invited Ruth's brothers to help their sister, was to clean up the house for four days, then move Ruth to a senior community where assistance and social interaction with same-age individuals would be possible every day to maintain Ruth's mental health and physical health. Ruth's "despicable duo brothers," after Ruth's son had to depart for his professional conference (remember, he waited three days for the arrival of the delinquent, arrogant, selfish "despicable duo brothers" to arrive three days after the planned house-cleaning start date, all because they went to a University of California Berkeley versus Stanford University football game instead of showing up to love and support their sister through their work and acts of kindness as had been scheduled and planned by Ruth's son and Ruth's "despicable duo brothers," thus subtracting three full days from the help their sister would have otherwise received).

In summary, they worked three days, one day beyond the extremely hard two days of house clutter and cleaning that Ruth's son labored through, then conspired in an indolent, very lazy, sluggish, and evil way to leave Ruth alone by herself in a now empty house, and without the desire or ability of Ruth to realistically maintain her home, pay her property tax and income tax each year, or even pay her utility and trash bills, thus choosing willfully to ensure that their sister would suffer without heat or air conditioning, without healthy medications or food, and without a clean and healthy home and bedroom (as it turned out, for the next seven years), ultimately leading to their sister's rapid mental and physical health decline and rapid deterioration for the next seven years of neglect, all enabled and facilitated by Ruth's unloving, sinister, and "despicable duo brothers." Her brothers conspired successfully, to convince their sister Ruth to ignore and reject her loving son's original plan and intent, which both Ruth's brothers initially agreed to in order to help her transition into a loving and supportive senior community where Ruth could be guaranteed to receive daily medications she required so that her mind and body would not rapidly decline and deteriorate due to loneliness, depression, anxiety, fiscal irresponsibility due to memory deficits and isolation (due to no possible visitors to Ruth's home due to the filthy, cluttered, and "public health hazard" home condition in which she was living (more accurately "surviving in") and which Ruth could no longer effectively manage and maintain, being unable or unwilling to reliably pay her utility bills to maintain functioning electricity and flowing water in her toilets and sinks due to her inability or unwillingness to seek and obtain professional plumbing work when necessary, and later, it was learned Ruth had stopped paying taxes for the next seven years after having been abandoned and neglected by her ungodly and unloving brothers), all ensured and guaranteed (the house was, again, filled to the ceiling in every room over the next seven years of Ruth's agony and associated rapid mental and physical health deterioration and decline, as reliably predicted by her son, and sadly and very disappointingly planned and premeditated by Ruth's "scumbag brothers" or, also known as "the dastardly duo" brothers.

The "despicable duo brothers" of Ruth, as if throwing Ruth's son under the bus and making the son the scapegoat for their neglect, abuse, and irresponsible support, management, and care for their very own sibling, their sister, these two selfish, lazy, atheist, and stingy (Ruth's twin stole or embezzled $4500.00 from Ruth's bank account, facilitated by Ruth's youngest atheist brother who stole the money from Ruth's bank account and gave it to his brother to pay for his plane tickets for a "football game trip" to California from Florida, without the consent or permission from Ruth's son, who was her financial power of attorney, thus to be informed of all financial transactions, and determine if approval of the intended use of funds is appropriate, which he would **never** have approved of (twin agreed to come volunteer, like the son of Ruth, without payment to help Ruth).

The atheist, "alcohol and illicit drugs abuser," youngest brother of the "despicable duo brothers" of Ruth, was the most evil and sinister criminal of the two lazy and unethical, unhelpful brothers to their loving and Godly sister who greatly needed their help and assistance but was not only let down, but betrayed and stabbed in the back! Atheist, alcohol/drug abuser brother, neglected, along with his brother, who conspired with him, their sister for seven years (after their late arrival, short house clean up, smear of Ruth's son's reputation and intent to help his mother, then rapid but extended 7-year abandonment of their sister to ensure, as their plan was, that her brain would be devastated when they returned seven years later, at which time the youngest brother sold his sister's home, hid all the money in his financial accounts, investment accounts, and the accounts of his family members, including his wife and his two sons, all without informing Ruth's son of these dastardly actions of evil intent and purpose. Ruth's son shared the role of financial power of attorney for Ruth. Thus, all these actions should not have occurred (never) and definitely not without the permission and approval of Ruth's son, who would have never authorized these criminal, inappropriate activities and actions. Shortly after embezzling or stealing all the proceeds of Ruth's home sale and hiding the funds effectively in multiple accounts of his family members, he rightly, justly, and most likely as an immediate verdict from God, unexpectedly died.

This same thief and atheist was so evil and arrogant that he wrote a book promoting atheism, apparently an effort to recruit more miserable persons into his negative, distorted, hostile, corrupt, and evil view of this life and world, so he could not, perhaps, feel so depressed and condemned and guilty for his unforgivable sins (forgivable to Christians, of course, but perhaps God had His limits as to how long and how many evil, dark, dastardly, demeaning sins He could tolerate from this same one evil human being, that were all being perpetrated against his own family members, e.g., his very own sister, Ruth, and Ruth's youngest son.

This "anti-role model, anti-mentor atheist father and youngest brother and greatest embezzler, thief, and traitor" to Ruth and Ruth's youngest son was definitively the most evil of the infamous "despicable duo" or "dastardly duo" brothers, so sad indeed! "The truth is sometimes harrowing and extremely painful to relate to and to hear, but it is always the most vital and enlightening teaching any human can hope and wish for!"

Ruth, being the loving and benevolent soul and Godly woman she had been since birth, encouraged both her children to not only attend but to happily rejoice and celebrate the marriages of all her siblings and cousins, and second cousins, and, similarly, also respect these relatives by attending all their funerals. Ruth's children abided by these rules or guidelines throughout their lives out of respect and admiration for their loving and angelic role-model mother sent to them by God's grace.

Unlike Ruth, who was a Godly and angelic mentor and fervent supporter of all her immediate family members and extended family members, and cousins, uncles, and aunts, her "two dastardly duo" brothers, abused, embezzled money from, disrespected, neglected, abandoned, and dishonored both Ruth and her entire family (including both her children) for almost sixty years. Ruth's "Two Dastardly Duo Brothers," in contrast, taught their children neither to respect nor honor or cherish their loving cousins during good and bad periods of life, including graduations, weddings, and other special or extremely significant life events, including funerals of their fellow cousins and family members.

Ruth's twin brother, Judas, taught his children, by his own selfish and traitor-like actions and example, how to never visit, love, or support your twin sibling and sister, a discouraging and downcast lesson they learned with great precision. Judas and his selfish and inconsiderate spouse lived on the East Coast of the United States their entire life and raised their children (one boy and one girl) there. For the first half of the inconsiderate life they lived in New England or the Northern part of the East Coast of the United States of America. They subsequently, after Judas suffered a heart attack or myocardial infarction, moved to Florida during their retirement years.

When God blessed Ruth with two children of her own, born approximately two years apart, one would naturally expect that a caring, loving, and supportive twin sibling would frequently visit, love, cherish, encourage, guide, and support the children of their fraternal twin sibling, sister Ruth, in this specific case. However, Judas lived up to his "traitor" name and reputation in every imaginable respect.

In the nearly sixty years that Judas was the maternal uncle to Ruth's two loving and God-respecting children, Judas and his enabling, downcast, selfish spouse, visited the home of Ruth and her children less than five times in the first score (twenty years), of Ruth's children's life. In the subsequent twoscore (forty years) of Ruth's children's lives, traitor Judas, brother of angelic Ruth, failed to visit either of Ruth's children in their homes or hometowns for the the remainder of evil Judas's life, and topped off by his dastardly behavior toward his loving twin sister by embezzling just under $5000.00 from his sister's estate, by having Ruth's youngest and most despicable substance-abusing and alcohol-abusing youngest, Satan-worshipping atheist antichrist-like brother, illegitimately write an unauthorized (Ruth's son was the financial power of attorney for his mother when she needed assistance near the end of her life), from Ruth's account without informing Ruth's son of this unauthorized check given to Judas. Judas used this approximately $5,000 check to fraudulently pay off his (unauthorized) travel expenses, including his plane ticket costs and his (unauthorized) football game ticket costs when he lied to Ruth's son, and said he would volunteer to join Ruth's son and Ruth's youngest brother to meet at Ruth's home, clean up the home, plan to sell the home, then move Ruth to a senior community where Ruth's mental, physical, social, and spiritual health could be maintained with consistency in this more supportive environment, which all three individuals agreed Ruth would benefit from when they planned the volunteer assistance trip to Ruth's home, which was in total clutter, disrepair, without functioning sinks, toilets, and without electricity because Ruth had not been able to successfully live alone, in a healthy, responsible, and safe manner, in recent years, as confirmed by her neglecting to pay many necessary bills that were required to live healthy, alone but happy, and successfully, and to maintain and ensure her zenith health, happiness, and serenity.

During this darkest and most desperate time of need in Ruth's life in which she needed the utmost sincerity and love from her siblings (fraternal twin and youngest brother), and her loving son, Ruth, was betrayed in the darkest and most disappointing manner by both her siblings.

Thomas, Ruth's youngest atheist, alcohol, and substance-abusing brother, and his wife, Monica, conspired with Ruth's twin brother and traitor, Judas, to completely sabotage the plan Ruth's son had devised and organized to help his mother depart from the (public health department "condemned residence", deemed not fit to live in due to its health hazards) house she could no longer afford, manage, maintain, and live in due to her inability to manage and maintain the functionality of her home, which was now much too large and expensive for her to heat, cool, perform necessary maintenance on plumbing or electricity problems, or seek remedies when necessary to maintain the functional status of her telephone line, all which occurred at random times throughout the years and which Ruth no longer had the judgment, energy, ability, or intent to pay the bills or seek the appropriate professional assistance when these "larger than life" problems occurred and destroyed, abolished, and devastated her will, intent, and ability to perform standard and health-preserving "activities of daily living" successfully.

One such example was the finding that, during hot summers, Ruth was forced, at least in her own mind or perception, to sleep outside at night, under the walnut tree in the backyard because she had stopped paying her utility and electricity bills, thus she had no electricity, and her air-conditioning unit was not functional, in addition to not having any functional water in her toilets (all clogged) and showers (plumbing problems), and no working bathroom or kitchen sinks with water. Ruth was in dire need of help and support and in a state of great distress.

In this setting of dire circumstances, which Ruth's son cared enough about to explore and shockingly discover, on his own and with no assistance from Ruth's brothers, and learning about his loving mother, who was suffering greatly, but at the same time, unwilling to change her lifelong philosophy of "not being a complainer," and despite Ruth's son living almost 350 miles away from his mother in a different city, Ruth's son ultimately also shockingly discovered and encountered the genuinely evil and Lucifer-like souls (or lack of souls, more accurately) of Ruth's sibling brothers.

Despite Ruth's son's in-person meeting with Ruth's brothers and his informing them of Ruth's unacceptable and extremely unhealthy current living situation, with no running water in her toilets or showers or sinks and no electricity for heating and cooling of the home, and no functioning lights or refrigerators without electricity due to non-payment of all bills, Ruth's brothers showed no compassion or adult-like responsible behavior whatsoever. While Ruth's son thought he appropriately reached out to Ruth's brothers for their love and support of their sister, all in order to move Ruth into a healthier living environment and community, and love and assist Ruth in her time of greatest need, both Ruth's brothers got a dagger out and stabbed Ruth in the back, figuratively, instead of being loving and compassionate, faithful brothers to Ruth and Ruth's son.

The plan that was devised and organized by Ruth's son and agreed to by Ruth's fraternal twin brother Judas and Ruth's ungodly youngest brother, who was the God-doubting, God-deficient Thomas, was for everyone to volunteer and travel at their own expense to Ruth's hometown and home, arriving on Friday, then clean out and clean up Ruth's home on Friday, Saturday, Sunday, Monday, and Tuesday, and have Ruth stay at her Registered Nurse friend's home during the cleaning of Ruth's home, then find a healthy, supportive senior community and living situation where Ruth could then move to and move in, enabling her to talk with and socialize successfully with others who were approximately in or near Ruth's age group and where she could make many friends, participate in organized senior community events, hobbies, and special activities such as concerts and group trips, and most importantly, receive assistance in healthy "activities of daily living," all without the stresses of financial obligations and payments, which were to be taken care of by Ruth's son, who voluntarily took on this obligation and commitment to his loving mother, all in order to promote, support, and ensure, to the greatest extent possible, the future health and the happiness of his lovely, Angelic, yet aging mother.

What actually happened was truly devastating to Ruth's Godly spiritual health, mental health, physical health, social health, and "thanks" to Ruth's two evil brothers, resulted in Ruth's loving sons being falsely accused (God later judged these actions and "executed" his sentence of both these "Dastardly Duo" brothers of Ruth) of being "unfaithful to and abandoning their loving mother" when, in reality, no one on this earth loved Ruth more than her two sons, who were never unfaithful to her nor ever abandoned her, nor would ever even consider these evil aspirations or actions. This unbelievably evil sin of distraction and deception of Ruth, mentally vulnerable and gullible due to years of unnecessary stress she endured from both her unfaithful and unloving husband and abandonment and neglect by her two brothers, inflicted upon Ruth by both her supposedly trustworthy (but not in reality), brothers, a sin for which both of Ruth's evil brothers will one day surely be severely punished for, judged harshly for, and suffer eternal damnation for.

This eternal damnation, and actually, in retrospect, damnation that God almost certainly inflicted on both brothers shortly after their mistreatment of their loving and faithful sister, who wrongly thought she could trust her brothers more than her most loving, devoted, faithful, and eternally loyal sons, was swift and efficiently executed by God, who had already been supremely let down and discouraged by what He observed in both brother's selfish and ungodly behavior throughout their lives, in their own families, and concerning how they both treated their sisters, Ruth and her older sister, Jane, who were both worthy of so much love and respect from their brothers, yet never even came close to feeling or receiving the love and respect they earned and deserved as a result of their Godliness and support of their brothers, despite never receiving equivalent love and respect from their "anti-Christ-like brothers." In fact, both brothers sealed their destiny, which was an eternal vacation to and in hell, and even booked early "first-class" flights to their destinations, specifically as a result of their evil and deceptive intentions and unloving actions that broke the spirit of both Ruth and her two sons, who intended to help their mother by recruiting the assistance of Ruth's brothers, not to harm and neglect her for the next seven years (the "end result" of Ruth's brothers' decision not to correctly transition their sister to a practical, feasible, and supportive senior living community for senior citizens who have demonstrated, in one or multiple ways and manners, such as in Ruth's case, that they could no longer care for themselves, independently, and in their own home without outside assistance and monitoring).

In essence, and to make a long and drawn-out, sad story shorter and succinct, the plan for "three responsible adult males (Ruth's two brothers and Ruth's youngest son), to assist and support Ruth in a Godly and responsible manner was a complete failure due to the sabotage of the entire plan by both brothers of Ruth. Incidentally, Ruth's oldest son also very much wanted to help Ruth during this trip and mission to help his loving mother, but was tied up with other commitments and serious obligations to fulfill and complete in another town more 600 miles away, and unable to assist his mother during this particular trip, but surely would have helped his mother, Ruth, if it was at all possible for him to be there this scheduled and intended "week of grace, mercy, and Godly support of Ruth by her siblings (e.g., "the dastardly duo") and her loving son.." Instead of following the concise, efficient, and what would have been the most wise and Godly plan of spending Friday through Tuesday, five days total, cleaning their sister's home and preparing for its sale to support and finance the necessary new senior citizen living community that Ruth was in need of, and rightfully was being encouraged to move into, in order to maintain her health, Ruth's two brothers chose instead to embezzle funds from Ruth's bank accounts, pay off their travel costs with these embezzled funds, and even go to Cal Berkeley versus Stanford University college football game on the first three days of this planned missionary trip to help their sister in dire need of their help, to optimize her future physical, mental, social, and spiritual health.

Because Ruth's son showed up Friday morning as planned and scheduled, but Ruth's brothers showed up three days late; the timeline of the project was essentially destroyed and made impractical and impossible. Ruth's son had to leave, as planned, on Wednesday to a professional continuing education meeting, and when he left, after days of intense cleaning of his mother's house, the two evil sibling brothers of Ruth, to disguise and hide their evil acts of embezzling money from Ruth's banks to play together at a college football game, as part of the audience, then purposely miss three-fifths of the planned days of cleaning their sister's home, decided they could save face by telling Ruth that they loved her so much that they would allow her to stay in her home alone, for the next seven years, as it turned out, without moving Ruth to a healthier living environment and senior social and supportive community, and concomitantly, then vilified Ruth's son by telling their sister that he no longer loved her or cared for her and simply wanted to move her out of her home "for no good reason," then further (and sinfully) coerced Ruth to call her youngest son while at his out-of-state professional education conference, and (they dictated for Ruth what she should say over the phone), told Ruth to say, "Please never come back to this house for its clean-up or any other reason, as you are not welcome here anymore." If ever there was an unforgivable sin to be committed by two siblings toward their fellow sister, this sin of lying and attempting to have their sister abandon her youngest and Godly son, for evil and untrue "made up" reasons, taking advantage of their sister who was already mentally compromised, was an act of Satan. Thereafter, God acted promptly to punish each of these "Dastardly Duo" "brothers" (evil saboteurs and traitors are more descriptive and accurate) in distinct yet equally righteous ways that God saw fit and just.

Ruth's evil brothers later revealed that their intent had been to "let their sister's mental health deteriorate to a progressively more severe state, at which point it would be easier for them to move her into a memory/dementia care facility," and, disappointingly, with sinister intent, to drain and embezzle money out of all her bank accounts over the next seven years (which the "dastardly duo brothers (and siblings)" accomplished with Satan's assistance), then clean up her home again (as it turned out, sadly, seven years later), sell her home, hide the money in their own retirement accounts, then use up her long-term care insurance for her admission into a dementia patient memory care facility, all of which they successfully and sinfully planned in a premeditated way, implemented, and achieved with great sinister success for them, Thomas and Judas, but resulted in the, figuratively speaking, backstabbing and functional murder of their sister by both her brothers, and the simultaneous or concomitant destruction or devastation of Ruth's loving relationship with both her sons, as a result of their (the "dastardly duo brothers (and siblings)"), lies told to Ruth about how both her sons had chosen to abandon her (again, the truth being the exact opposite), so she should only trust them now and never listen to or accept offered help or assistance from either of her two (loving and Godly), sons!

Judas, Ruth's fraternal twin brother, was an excessively harsh father, who was also verbally abusive to his son and younger daughter throughout their childhood. He was also a poor role model, drinking alcohol frequently in front of his young and impressionable children. Judas, through his harsh, angry, and punitive nature as a father to his two children, essentially portrayed a father who was both unkind and brutally judgmental, which both his children later rebelled against, especially in grammar school, high school, and during the university education years. Judas's oldest child, his son, rebelled intensely in response to his overbearing, unkind, ungodly, hypercritical, and unsupportive father during his university education years, heavily indulging in multiple substance abuse (illicit drug abuse) and excessive alcohol abuse.

Judas's son's first marriage later ended in divorce. This son later met someone who would become his second wife and who could better tolerate who he is, and was in the past, during his university education years of drug and alcohol abuse! Judas's daughter intensely rebelled at an even younger age against and as a result of her father's unloving, unkind, hypercritical, and unsupported nature. His daughter was a very heavy smoker in grammar school, high school, and during her four years of university education, and engaged in tobacco abuse many years after college, at which time she also became a significant abuser of alcohol and eventually ended up as a very unhealthy and morbidly obese individual with innumerable serious health conditions and diseases.

Judas was consistently, throughout his life, a selfish, judgmental, unkind, unloving man to his children, his siblings, and his (supposedly a devout Catholic man), God, whom he repeatedly betrayed and disrespected by his inappropriate and unkind, unloving, selfishness, and unwillingness to care for and support others, similar to how he wished to be cared for and supported, e.g., by his wife, children, and siblings who shared their love for Judas repeatedly and through so many of their actions throughout Judas's life, which he reciprocated in either his attitude, perspective, or actions toward his children and siblings.

Multiple examples exist to demonstrate the selfish and narcissistic behavior of Judas toward his siblings, cousins, and other family members.

One such example is that of Ruth's sons attending the marriage of Judas and his wife, and the initial weddings of his children, and frequently visiting his home, despite living approximately 3000 miles from Judas's home.

Yet when the time came that Ruth's child was to be married, Judas and his narcissist spouse and children, all of like-mind (selfish, unloving, unsupportive, atheist, satan worshipers), refused to accept the invitation or attend Ruth's son's wedding, as was the exact same situation with Ruth's youngest brother who was an atheist, drug abuser, and alcohol abuser. Ruth's youngest brother was an arrogant, unGodly, and vane "man," e.g., despicable human, with similar (in sinister character) narcissist wife and children who care only about themselves and no one else, and who were also invited to Ruth's son's wedding, yet their children never even considered attending the wedding of their cousin.

The "dastardly duo brothers," the children, grandchildren, and all other family members who only took the Godly love, kindness, care, compassion, mercy, grace, and forgiveness provided during the angelic earthly life journeys, en route to their eternal spiritual destination and reunion with God, of Jane and her younger sister Ruth, concisely summarized as "Two Sisters, The Dynamic Duo, Pilgrimage To Eternity," would never be given back or returned in like-kind to these two Angels sent from God to tolerate, care for, support, be role models for, and love without conditions or prerequisites or postrequisites, luckily, parameters and conditions both Angels accepted and embraced wholeheartedly as a result of the inner strength and powerful Godly spirit and soul ingrained within them, and gifted to them by God, their inspiration, creator, and heavenly, joyful reunion organizer!

This disdain and disrespect these two angels were destined to endure and persevere throughout their entire lives is eerily similar to what Jesus Christ endured and powered through to achieve his glorious and eternal destiny of forgiveness of sins of all humans "who know not what they do," again demonstrating unparalleled Godly love, as was bestowed by these two angels on their ungrateful, and even resentful, irresponsible, rebellious, and in several sad cases, atheist family members who were unwilling to return, in kind, the immense love given to them by their angelic two sisters.

Further enlightening examples, though myriad in number for the two sister angels, follow in the select few descriptions below, in which both angels were resilient and resistant to harsh mistreatment and abuse. Both these Angels, "Two Sisters, The Dynamic Duo," were powerful, wise, and strong, always knowing who they were as God's creations regardless of the neglect, abandonment, or disregard they unjustly were subjected to and relegated to by their unloving family spouses and siblings or other unappreciative friends (the last being absent and nonexistent throughout these two angels lives).

Just to clarify, however, both Angels had myriad friends and work colleagues who clearly saw the true, faithful, and Godly Angels that both women represented and lived their lives accordingly, despite their family members living up to the unimpressive reputation and concept denoted in the following cliché or popularly used phrase: "With friends (e.g., ungodly family members) like that, who needs enemies?"

Ruth outlived her elder sister Jane despite Ruth's many personal struggles, life stressors, and neglect and abandonment by her male siblings. Not surprisingly, nor unexpected from her traitor brothers, Ruth's brothers planned a memorial service and burial service for Jane, which not only excluded and never invited Ruth to her beloved elder sister's burial service, but also never notified Ruth's husband and children of the memorial service arrangements and services, and, to add insult to (emotional) injury, Ruth's brothers went as far as to actually lie about the exact dates of the memorial service when Ruth and her family found out that Ruth's youngest and most evil brother, all of a sudden, was planning a "road trip" with his family members in their recreational camper vehicle to the East Coast of the United States, including a visit to Claremont, New Hampshire, where Jane, Ruth, and their "Dastardly Duo Brothers" all grew up and were raised, from birth until they all departed upon high school graduation, off to distinct universities on the West Coast of the United States, specifically the state of California, where the four siblings (oldest to youngest), Jane, Ruth, Judas ("traitor"), and Thomas ("atheist, God-doubting") all attended their future respective universities to complete their higher education before embarking on their professional careers and lives, specifically at the University of Southern California, San Jose State University, University of California Berkeley, and (Florida University, never completed)/University of California Los Angeles/University of California San Francisco, respectively. Ruth and her loving family members, her husband, and two children were again heartbroken and deeply disturbed by her "Dastardly Duo Brothers," evil intent and resolve to enact yet another vicious crime and insult, figuratively, stabbing their Godly and loving sister, once again, not only in her back this time, but also straight through her heart and soul by this particular act of lunacy and pure evil, not even respecting their siblings right and intent to honor her elder sister, at and during her memorial and burial services, in their hometown of Claremont, New Hampshire. As a famous movie quote once said, "Stupid is as stupid does." In this specific ignoble, nefarious, odious, heinous, contemptible, execrable, diabolic, flagitious, egregious, peccable, fiendish, depraved, malevolent, and unholy conspiracy that was plotted out and planned to the most microscopic detail of deception and sabotage of the Godly and holy spirit of their sibling sister Ruth and her loving family members, these "dastardly duo brothers (note: no capitalization of this title is even remotely warranted)," and their consenting and conspiring family members, all with VIP life memberships in the clubs of: Antichrist, Beelzebub, Demon, Lucifer, Mephistopheles, Angel of Darkness, Apollyon, Archfiend, Diabolus, King of Hell, Prince of Darkness, The Evil Spirit and all conspiring family members also earned and achieved "Honors At Entrance" into these clubs mentioned above, an honor they very much deserved!

If this book were to be made into a movie in future years, the updated quote describing, concisely, this act of treachery toward both Jane, who would have insisted that her sister be not only included but a vital part of and speaker or orator at her (Jane) funeral service and burial ceremony, and the quote would concisely be characterized and communicated as follows: "Sinister is as Satan Does!"

While Ruth's youngest son acknowledges and respects the fact that God has the final say in all trials of and judgments and sentencing of evildoers, in God's omnipresent and outside the time spectrum, e.g., God's simultaneous view of all past, present, and future occurrences in the human time spectrum, court of Godly Justice, and will ultimately render his punishments for and to all individuals engaging in evil acts and deeds perpetrated on other humans who are all "God's creations and family members (e.g., every human being born on this Earth)," Ruth's youngest son, based on the Godly upbringing and fervor and desire for justice and equality for "all God's children and family members on earth," feels the need and desire to expose these acts of ungodly and evil intent, which were enacted and accomplished with satanic fervor and enthusiasm by those dastardly students or mentorees of their mentor in this world, Satan. All human beings may be educated and enlightened by learning of these evil acts and realizing that such acts will not go unpunished and that these perpetrators were promptly indicted and judgment "executed" (figuratively and literally, at least in one case) by God, their creator.

For all those readers who might surmise that this description of and characterization of the "Dastardly Duo Brothers" is unreasonable, unforgiving, or otherwise overly harsh, readers are always, of course, entitled to their own opinions, right or wrong, and Ruth's youngest son accepts and has embraced this fact of life. However, having not had the'disadvantage' of suffering one's whole life from the evil, traitor, and saboteur behavior of these two brothers toward their two Godly sisters, the reader should, at the very least, be open to the realization that their impression or opinion may not be one hundred percent accurate or correct, yet if they engender or possess the desire and proactive initiative to plant, fertilize, and water, a mustard seed worth of faith in the truth that this author is attempting to convey, for the Godly purpose of enlightening others as to the evil intent, purpose, and harmful actions of some humans (aka, "God's children), toward other family members and humans, all equal and vital creations and members by birth and requisite faith in God, their creator, that are desired and loved family members of God, their creator, then these scenarios, which educate and enlighten the reader will act as pillars of support and precautions "to them who have (Godly) ears to hear, or eyes to see, read, and interpret," such that they may benefit and remain safe and secure, kind and loving, all as a result of the precautions, warnings, and true stories that were strongly persevered by "Two Sisters, The Dynamic Duo, Pilgrimage To Eternity." During the darkest and most depressing or discouraging periods of their lives, "Two Sisters, The Dynamic Duo, Pilgrimage To Eternity" was possible as a result of God's guidance of these two Angelic sisters and the acquired life principles and guidance they pursued and learned throughout their existence. These "Two Sisters, The Dynamic Duo, Pilgrimage To Eternity" were the most resoundingly and astonishingly loving and supporting mentors of all ages, outside the human and earthly time spectrum, and should thus serve as an example of every human's potential to be amazing, angelic, and Godly mentors to all their fellow human beings, able to guide and protect all humans impeccably and flawlessly at all times, literally, and figuratively. God, their creator, made this possible for them and similarly makes their amazing and benevolent life performances possible for all human beings who are all equally respected and honored members of the worldwide family known as "God's children" or "humankind."

Note that in the last sentence of the previous paragraph, two essential words are keys to happiness in life on this planet, and the latter half of both these all-important words contain the same, identical word within the more prominent scope words recited, and these short words are reiterated twice in the last three words of this sentence. Was this by chance alone? The answer is obvious: no. However, it was perhaps (to be determined, again, by the reader), serendipitous! Kind is truly the word that describes God's purposeful intent for how all God's creations treat each other on a "daily and nightly" basis during their fleeting and ephemeral time of life and existence on planet Earth.

Judas, Ruth's fraternal twin brother and professional betrayer of his sisters, in addition to not attending Ruth's memorial service with his conspiring and complicit spouse went further to generate and stir up discontent and disappointment amongst all Ruth's family members, by discouraging and dissuading many of Ruth's East Coast of United States grammar school and high school classmates and friends, as well as family members and East Coast residents to attend her widely publicized (in local newspapers of Ruth's hometowns as a child and as an adult), memorial and burial services in Claremont, New Hampshire. Ruth's retired dental surgeon cousin, his wife, and Ruth's husband, disappointingly, made other activities their priorities on the scheduled, well in advance, date of Ruth's memorial and burial service ceremonies, a shocking and disturbing occurrence, but when entrenched in the love and strength and happiness of God, there is no human behavior that is allowed to or can disappoint the recipient of God's eternal love, kindness, peace, serenity, and happiness during this life, or in Ruth's case, shortly after this life, and in the midst of her undeniable and unstoppable "pilgrimage to eternity!"

Judas was the genuine example of an "anti-mentor" in this life to his entire family, though his younger brother, Thomas, competed hard to catch up to Judas's Lucifer and demonic example, and, at the end of Thomas's young life and premature death (though perhaps not premature in the eyes and judgment of God), finally caught up to and maybe even surpassed his elder brother's evilness and fraudulent deception of his family and friends by proposing or supposing (more accurately, impersonating) his being a "devout Catholic," when he was actually a hypocrite in every true sense of this word's definition: A person who claims or pretends to have certain beliefs about what is right and just but who behaves in a way or manner that disagrees with the basis and the intent of those beliefs.

When Ruth's two sons could have benefitted from the love and support of their uncle and mother's fraternal twin, Judas chose instead to abandon, ignore, and neglect them by not visiting them for nearly sixty consecutive years. Luckily and due to Ruth's Godly principles, teachings, actual Christian values and proactive Christian perspectives, attitudes, and supremely important, Christian actions and lifestyle (e.g., not overspending on expensive clothing or vanity-related expenses or items she neither required nor needed, despite her desires, in order to responsibly run the financial budget in the family and to thwart the indiscriminate and irresponsible spending habits of her selfish husband, who always placed his priorities and wishes over those of his Godly wife and two children, who fortunately were keen and admiring observers of their beautiful, kind, generous, wise mentor, listener, Godly example of "how to live life," known as their "loving mother Ruth."

An age-old adage that is relevant at this point is: "Children must always respect their parents." This concept, proverb, and teaching is encouraged throughout the Bible, the greatest book ever written. A conflict or dilemma, however, occurs in the life of every child and human being when they are a child, or later during their teenager years, or adulthood years, and they become enlightened about the positive and less-than-positive aspects, attitudes, intent, aspirations, motivations, and, most vital, behavior and actions in response to and toward the children and that particular parent's spouse.

A fine line is established and becomes apparent or visible when each child then uses their God-gifted brain, discretion, insight, intuition, keen powers of active listening and careful observation, wisdom, and enlightenment that follows daily "self-teaching," and "self-learning," in addition to education received by others' teachings and actions, learning from one's own errors and mistakes, as well as those from other individuals such as strangers, friends, or family members, that each child or adult comes into contact with throughout their progression through life. While no one would or should argue that children should not respect their parents, as even God directs everyone to perform this task to receive the full blessings of God during their lifetime, there does come a time in every child's or adult's life, at which point they reflect back on the behavior and actions of their parents, and must, thereafter, reconcile their innocent, uninformed, or uneducated youthful perspectives, with their now seasoned, and more informed and wise or enlightened perspective on life and proper or ideal parenting, which they may have may or may not have always experienced or realized on a daily basis, depending on the dispensed behavior and actions of their immature then later more wise and experienced parents, as is the case with all humans, as no human is born an expert parent with vast parenting experience, especially prior to the birth of their first (in a sense, experimental, and "trial and error"), child.

How, then, can book authors or movie screenplay writers "walk the fine line" of truthfully reviewing the performance and actions of each of their parents in order to accurately praise, acknowledge, encourage, and glorify the parent, in real-time or in retrospect, who is, or who had in the past during the raising of their children, excelled above and beyond God's guiding principles regarding good parenting performance and actions within the married couple's family, and similarly, accurately and truthfully admonish any less than perfect, or perhaps disappointing or inappropriately behaving parent (hopefully not worse, but we all know these situations do occur), who is, or who had in the past, during the raising of their children, demonstrated, or is currently demonstrating inattention or blatant or even informed and intentional disregard for God's guiding principles regarding good parenting performance and actions?

Enlightenment in this world can only result from the wise, truthful and honest accounts of the "pros and cons" of exceptional and Godly behavior and actions versus bad and ungodly behavior and actions. This revelation, in Ruth's youngest son's experience, results almost exclusively from the

God-given wisdom and discernment of those writers who have been gifted by God to impart God's wisdom through their writings, thus making them God's astute mentors to the world, and enabling them to inform, educate, or admonish, where appropriate, their fellow human beings and universal members of God's family, also known as humankind.

Judas, while failing repeatedly for nearly sixty years to generously encourage and praise the Godly aspirations, actions, and achievements of his twin sister's family and children, unbelievably encouraged and failed to admonish, at the same time, his youngest brother, who split off the Godly trail through life, and took his entire family down the devastating and depressing path of atheism, alcohol, and substance abuse, which, with Thomas as the head of his family, all his family members followed his life path to hell, without resistance or even second-guessing the valueless principles and lack of morality their father displayed on a daily basis. What is worse is that Judas, Thomas's older (and supposedly wiser and more Godly, but not in reality, brother), never once, effectively, or convincingly attempted to win over his younger brother from the pending depths of hell that Thomas was heading toward his entire life, culminating in his writing a manuscript promoting atheism, shortly after which he suddenly dropped dead without warning at a young and unexpectedly young age. Of another interesting note, not to be ignored or discounted for Thomas's premature and seemingly untimely early death was that he had, just before his death, as an atheist, obtained a California license (somehow) to marry his oldest son to his son's bride," despite not being affiliated with any church and not believing in God whatsoever. You can imagine the negative and depressing content of these ungodly wedding vows without any mention of God.

Ironically, while Judas neglected to attend the Godly wedding of Ruth's son, which occurred years before the wedding of Thomas's oldest son, when both weddings were located in California, and Judas and his complicit, fellow conspiring hypocrite religious wife and children all lived on the the opposite side of the United States on the East Coast, Judas shunned and abandoned Ruth's son's wedding by not attending, similar to his family's unloving, non-supportive actions throughout Ruth's life and the lives of her children, who, again, never were visited by Judas and his family members. Yet as soon as the youngest atheist brother of Judas, "God-Doubting and God-shunning Thomas" announced the planned marriage of his oldest son, and that Thomas would be applying for a (non-God-ordained minister) license such that Thomas could legally perform the marriage of his atheist son, Judas, the supposed "devout Catholic Christian" (not so much, or not at all in reality), then jumped on the news, immediately bought plane tickets, and made housing arrangements to attend the wedding, never even once playing the role of a Godly mentor and old brother who could have and should have, throughout his life, out of Godly love and respect for his younger brother, admonish his younger brother to seek out God and place his faith and the faith of his entire family in God his creator. Instead, Judas chose a cowardice approach to his younger brothers ill-advised and ungodly path through life, and similar to how Judas disrespected and abandoned any attempts to love and support his twin sister during her era of critical need for intervention to assist and fortify her mental and physical health, Judas chose again to pacify, deceive, and abandon those siblings in his life who most needed him and to whom he decided to pacify and thus devastate, via his lack of resolve, courage, and overwhelming cowardice and fraudulent, ungodly behavior and actions, which defied his false claims of being a devout Catholic Christian his whole life. In essence, Judas enabled, supported, and encouraged his younger brother, Thomas (via Judas's attitude, perspective, and actions), to pursue and successfully arrive at a doomed final destination in life, essentially over more than seventy years, enabling Thomas, his youngest atheist brother, to purchase, with Satan's credit card, a first class ticket to hell. Hell, quite assuredly, has accepted Thomas and celebrated his early arrival with a heated barbecue, serving up his Godly body and soul, which God gifted to him at his birth, as the main barbecue entrée. With any luck whatsoever, it is still Ruth's youngest son's hope and wish that Thomas received God's grace and mercy, despite his lifelong sins and disrespect for God his entire life, but this wish of good intent is only that, a wish of good intent.

However, the Bible teaches that God is a just and righteous God, and thus is not inclined or obligated to bestow grace and mercy on those children of God, who openly and intentionally rejected God as their creator, never repented of their personal sins and never demonstrated and put into action their faith in God, by converting and changing their ungodly perspective, attitude, and behavior into that of a traditional Christian, as described in great detail in the Bible, the greatest book ever written and given to humankind and mankind, as a gift from God to his created children.

The "Dastardly Duo Brothers," the children, grandchildren, and all other family members who only took the Godly love, kindness, care, compassion, mercy, grace, and forgiveness provided during the angelic earthly life journeys, enroute to their eternal spiritual destination, and reunion with God, of Jane and her younger sister Ruth, concisely summarized as "Two Sisters, The Dynamic Duo, Pilgrimage To Eternity," would never be given back or returned in like-kind to these two Angels sent from God to tolerate, care for, support, be role models for and love without conditions or prerequisites or postrequisites, luckily, parameters and conditions both Angels accepted and embraced wholeheartedly as a result of the inner strength and powerful Godly spirit and soul ingrained within them and gifted to them by God, their inspiration, creator, and heavenly, joyful reunion organizer!

This disdain and disrespect these two Angels were destined to endure and persevere throughout their entire lives is eerily similar to what Jesus Christ endured and powered through to achieve his glorious and eternal destiny of forgiveness of sins of all humans "who know not what they do," again demonstrating unparalleled Godly love, as was bestowed by these two angels on their ungrateful, and even resentful, irresponsible, rebellious, and in several sad cases, atheist family members who could not see fit to return the immense love given to them by their angelic two sisters.

Further enlightening examples, though myriad in number for the two sister Angels, follow in the select few descriptions below, in which both angels were resilient and resistant to harsh mistreatment or just Godly powerful and strong in always knowing who they were as God's creations regardless of the neglect, abandonment, or disregard they unjustly were relegated to by their unloving family member or other unappreciative friends.

Just to clarify, however, both Angels had myriad friends and work colleagues who clearly saw the faithful and Godly Angels that both women represented and lived their lives accordingly, despite their family members living up to the unimpressive reputation and concept denoted in the following cliché or popularly used phrase: "With friends (e.g., ungodly family members) like that, who needs enemies?"

Ruth outlived her elder sister Jane despite Ruth's many personal struggles, life stressors, and neglect and abandonment by her male siblings.

Not surprisingly, nor unexpected from her traitor brothers, Ruth's brothers planned a memorial service and burial service for Jane, which not only excluded and never invited Ruth to her beloved elder sister's burial service, but also never notified Ruth's husband and children of the memorial service arrangements and services, and, to add insult to (emotional) injury, Ruth's brothers went as far to actually lie about the exact dates of the memorial service when Ruth and her family found out that Ruth's youngest and most evil brother, all of a Suddenly, he was planning a "road trip" with his family members to the East Coast of the United States, including a visit to Claremont, New Hampshire, where Jane, Ruth, and their "Dastardly Duo Brothers" all grew up and were raised, from birth until they all departed upon high school graduation, off to distinct universities on the West Coast of the United States, specifically the state of California, where the four siblings (oldest to youngest), Jane, Ruth, ("traitor") Judas, and ("atheist, God-doubting") Thomas, all attended their future respective universities to complete their higher education before embarking on their professional careers and lives, specifically at the University of Southern California, San Jose State University, University of California Berkeley, and (Florida University, never completed)/University of California Los Angeles/University of California San Francisco, respectively. Ruth and her loving family members, husband, and two children included, were again heartbroken and deeply disturbed by her "Dastardly Duo Brothers," evil intent and resolve to enact yet another evil crime and insult, figuratively, stabbing their Godly and loving sister, once again, not only in her back this time, but also straight through her heart and soul by this particular act of lunacy and pure evil, not even respecting their sibling's right and intent to honor her elder sister, at and during her memorial and burial service in their hometown of Claremont, New Hampshire. As a famous movie quote once said, "Stupid is as stupid does." In this specific ignoble, nefarious, odious, heinous, contemptible, execrable, diabolic, flagitious, egregious, peccable, fiendish, depraved, malevolent and unholy conspiracy plotted out and planned to the most microscopic detail of deception and sabotage of the Godly and holy spirit of their sibling sister Ruth and her loving family members, these "Dastardly Duo Brothers," and their consenting and conspiring family members, all with VIP life memberships in the clubs of Antichrist, Beelzebub, Demon, Lucifer, Mephistopheles, Angel of Darkness, Apollyon, Archfiend, Diabolus, King of Hell, Prince of Darkness, The Evil Spirit, and all conspiring family members also achieving "Honors At Entrance" into these above-mentioned clubs, an honor they earned and very much deserved! If this book was to be made into a movie in the future years, the updated quote describing this act of treachery concisely toward both Jane, who would have insisted that her sister be not only included but a vital part of and speaker or orator at her (Jane's) funeral service and burial ceremony and the quote would concisely be characterized and communicated as follows: "Sinister is as Satan does!"

While Ruth's youngest son acknowledges and respects the fact that God has the final say in all trials of and judgments and sentencing of evildoers, in God's omnipresent and outside the time spectrum, e.g., God's simultaneous view of all past, present, and future occurrences in the human time spectrum, court of Godly Justice, and will ultimately render his punishments for and to all individuals engaging in evil acts and deeds perpetrated on other humans who are all "God's creations and family members (e.g., every human being born on this Earth)," Ruth's youngest son, based on the Godly upbringing and fervor and desire for justice and equality for "all God's children and family members on earth" feels the need and desire to expose these acts of ungodly and evil intent, which were enacted and accomplished with satanic fervor and enthusiasm by those dastardly students or mentorees of their mentor in this world, Satan.

For all those readers who might surmise that this description of and characterization of the "Dastardly Duo Brothers" is unreasonable, unforgiving or otherwise overly harsh, readers are always, of course, entitled to their own opinions, right or wrong, and Ruth's youngest son accepts and has embraced this fact of life. However, having not had the 'disadvantage' of suffering one's whole life from the evil, traitor, and saboteur behavior of these two brothers toward their two Godly sisters, the reader should, at the very least, be open to the realization that their impression or opinion may not be one hundred percent accurate or correct, yet if they engender or possess the desire and proactive initiative to plant, fertilize, and water a mustard seed worth of faith in the truth that this author is attempting to convey, for the Godly purpose of enlightening others as to the evil intent, purpose, and harmful actions of some humans (aka, "God's children) toward other family members and humans, all equal and vital creations and members by birth and requisite faith in God, their creator, that are desired and loved family members of God, their creator, then these scenarios which educate and enlighten the reader will act as pillars of support and precautions "to them who have (Godly) ears to hear, or eyes to see, read, and interpret," such that they may benefit and remain safe and secure, kind and loving, all as a result of the precautions and warnings, and true stories that Ruth's youngest son experienced first-hand, and luckily, but more importantly, strongly persevered through, especially during darkest and most otherwise depressing or discouraging eras as a result of Ruth's youngest son's acquired life principles and guidance, made possible by the most valuable mentors, educators, and trailblazers (who were on their own pilgrimage to eternity, hint, hint), throughout life, namely "Two Women, The Dynamic Duo, Pilgrimage To Eternity," and most resoundingly and astonishingly loving and supporting Mentor of all ages, outside the human and earthly time spectrum, thus able to guide and protect all humans in an impeccable and flawless manner at all times, literally and figuratively, God the creator of all members of the family known as humankind.

Note that in the last sentence of the previous paragraph, two essential words are keys to happiness in life on this planet, and the latter half of both these all-important words contain the same, identical word within the larger scope words recited, and these short words are reiterated twice in the last three words of this sentence. Was this by chance alone? The answer is obvious: no. However, it was perhaps (to be determined, again, by the reader) serendipitous! Kind is indeed the word that describes God's purposeful intent for how all God's creations treat each other on a daily and nightly basis during their fleeting and ephemeral time of life and existence on planet Earth.

Judas, Ruth's fraternal twin brother and professional betrayer of his sisters, besides not attending Ruth's memorial service with his conspiring and complicit spouse, went further to generate and stir up discontent and disappointment amongst all Ruth's family members, by discouraging and dissuading many of Ruth's East Coast of United States grammar school and high school classmates and friends, as well as family members and East Coast residents to attend her widely publicized (in local newspapers of Ruth's hometowns as a child and as an adult), memorial and burial services in Claremont, New Hampshire. Ruth's retired dental surgeon cousin, his wife, and Ruth's husband, disappointingly, made other activities their priorities on the scheduled, well in advance, date of Ruth's memorial and burial service ceremonies, a shocking and disturbing occurrence, but when entrenched in the love and strength and happiness of God, there is no human behavior that is allowed to or can disappoint the recipient of God's eternal love, kindness, peace, serenity, and happiness during this life, or in Ruth's case, shortly after this life, and in the midst of her undeniable and unstoppable "pilgrimage to eternity!"

Judas was the "greatest" (most nefarious) example of an "anti-mentor" in this life to his entire family, though his younger brother, Thomas, competed hard to catch up to Judas's Lucifer and demonic example, and, at the end of Thomas young life and premature death (though perhaps not early in the eyes and judgment of God), finally caught up to and maybe even surpassed his elder brother's evilness, fraudulent deception of his family and friends by proposing or supposing (more accurately, impersonating) his being a "devout Catholic," when he was actually a hypocrite, in every true sense of this word's definition: A person who claims or pretends to have certain beliefs about what is right and just, but who behaves in a way or manner that disagrees with the basis and intent of those beliefs.

When Ruth's two sons could have benefitted from the love and support of their uncle and mother's fraternal twin, Judas chose instead to abandon, ignore, and neglect them by not visiting them for nearly sixty consecutive years. Luckily and due to Ruth's Godly principles, teachings, actual Christian values and proactive Christian perspectives, attitudes, and supremely important, Christian actions and lifestyle (e.g., not overspending on expensive clothing or vanity-related expenses or items she neither required nor needed, despite her desires, to responsibly run the financial budget in the family, and to thwart the indiscriminate and irresponsible spending habits of her selfish husband, who always placed his priorities and wishes over those of his Godly wife and two children, who fortunately were keen and admiring observers of their beautiful, kind, generous, wise mentor, listener, Godly example of "how to live life," known as their "loving mother Ruth."

An age-old adage that is relevant at this point, at least in the Ruth's youngest son's mind is: "Children must always respect their parents." This concept, proverb, and teaching is encouraged throughout the Bible, the greatest book ever written. A conflict or dilemma, however, occurs in the life of every child and human being when they are a child, or later during their teenager years, or adulthood years, and they become enlightened about the positive and less-than-positive aspects, attitudes, intent, aspirations, motivations, and, most vital, behavior and actions in response to and toward the children and that particular parent's spouse.

A fine line is established and becomes apparent or visible when each child then uses their God-gifted brain, discretion, insight, intuition, keen powers of active listening and careful observation, and wisdom and enlightenment that follows daily "self-teaching," education by others' teachings and actions, learning from one's own errors and mistakes, as well as those from other individuals such as strangers, friends, or family members, that each child or adult comes into contact with throughout their progression through life. While no one would or should argue that children should not respect their parents, as even God directs everyone to perform this task to receive the full blessings of God during their lifetime, there does come a time in every child's or adult's life, at which point they reflect back on the behavior and actions of their parents, and must, thereafter, reconcile their innocent, uninformed, or uneducated youthful perspectives, with their now seasoned, and more informed and wise or enlightened perspective on life and proper or ideal parenting, which they may have may or may not have always experienced or realized daily, depending on the dispensed behavior and actions of their immature then later more wise and experienced parents, as is the case with all humans, as no human is born an expert parent with vast parenting experience, especially before the birth of their first (in a sense, experimental, and "trial and error"), child.

How then can a book authors or movie screenplay writers "walk the fine line" of truthfully reviewing the performance and actions of each of their parents to accurately praise, acknowledge, encourage, and glorify the parent, in real-time or in retrospect, who is, or who had in the past during the raising of their children, excelled above and beyond God's guiding principles regarding good parenting performance and actions within the married couple's family, and similarly, accurately and truthfully admonish any less than perfect, or perhaps disappointing or inappropriately behaving parent (hopefully not worse, but we all know these situations do occur), who is currently demonstrating or who had, in the past, during the raising of their children, showed inattention or blatant or even informed and intentional disregard for God's guiding principles regarding good parenting performance and actions?

Enlightenment in this world can only result from the wise, truthful and honest accounts of the "pros and cons" of excellent and Godly behavior and actions versus bad and ungodly behavior and actions. This revelation, in Ruth's youngest son's experience, results almost exclusively from the God-given wisdom and discernment of those writers who have been gifted by God to impart God's wisdom through their writings, thus making them God's astute mentors to the world, and enabling them to inform, educate, or admonish, where appropriate, their fellow human beings and universal members of God's family, also known as humankind or mankind.

Judas, while failing repeatedly for nearly sixty years to generously encourage and praise the Godly aspirations, actions, and achievements of his twin sister's family and children, unbelievably encouraged and failed to admonish, at the same time, his youngest brother, who split off the Godly trail through life, and took his entire family down the devastating and depressing path of atheism, alcohol, and substance abuse, which, with Thomas as the head of his family, all his family members followed his life path to hell, without resistance or even second-guessing the valueless principles and lack of morality their father displayed on a daily basis. What is worse is that Judas, Thomas's older (and supposedly wiser and more Godly, but not in reality, brother), never once, effectively, or convincingly attempted to win over his younger brother from the pending depths of hell, that Thomas was heading toward his entire life, culminating in his writing a manuscript promoting atheism, shortly after which he suddenly dropped dead without warning to him or his whole family at a young and seemingly premature (at least to his family members) age. Of another interesting note, not to be ignored or discounted for Thomas's "premature" and seemingly untimely early death, was that he had, just before his death, as an atheist, obtained a California license (somehow) to marry his oldest son to his son's bride," despite not being affiliated with any church and not believing in God whatsoever. You can imagine the negative and depressing content of these ungodly wedding vows without any mention of God.

Ironically, while Judas neglected to attend the Godly wedding of Ruth's son, which occurred years before the wedding of Thomas's oldest son, when both weddings were located in California, and Judas and his complicit, fellow conspiring hypocrite religious wife and children all lived on the opposite side of the United States on the East Coast, Judas shunned and abandoned Ruth's son's wedding by not attending, similar to his family's unloving, non-supportive actions throughout Ruth's life and the lives of her children, who, again, never were visited by Judas and his family members. Yet as soon as the youngest atheist brother of Judas, "God-Doubting and God-shunning Thomas" announced the planned marriage of his oldest son, and that Thomas would be applying for a (non-God-ordained minister) license such that Thomas could legally perform the marriage of his atheist son, Judas, the supposed "devout Catholic Christian" (not so much, or not at all in reality), then jumped on the news, immediately bought plane tickets, and made housing arrangements to attend the wedding, never even once playing the role of a Godly mentor and old brother who could have and should have, throughout his life, out of Godly love and respect for his younger brother, admonish his younger brother to seek out God and place his faith and the faith of his entire family in God his creator. Instead, Judas chose a cowardice approach to his younger brothers ill-advised and ungodly path through life, and similar to how Judas disrespected and abandoned any attempts to love and support his twin sister during her era of critical need for intervention to assist and fortify her mental and physical health, Judas chose again to pacify, deceive, and abandon those siblings in his life who most needed him and to whom he decided to pacify and thus devastate, via his lack of resolve, courage, and overwhelming cowardice and fraudulent, ungodly behavior and actions, which defied his false claims to have been a devout Catholic Christian his whole life. In essence, Judas enabled, supported, and encouraged his younger brother, Thomas (via Judas's attitude, perspective, and actions), to pursue and successfully arrive at a doomed final destination in life, essentially over more than seventy years, enabling Thomas, his youngest atheist brother, to purchase with Satan's credit card, a first-class ticket to hell. Hell, quite assuredly, has accepted Thomas and celebrated his early arrival with a heated barbecue, serving up his Godly body and soul, which God gifted to him at his birth, as the main barbecue entrée. With any luck whatsoever, it is still Ruth's youngest son's hope and wish that Thomas receives or received God's grace and mercy despite his lifelong sins and disrespect for God his entire life, but this wish of good intent is only that, a wish of good intent. However, the Bible teaches that God is a just and righteous God, and thus is not inclined or obligated to bestow grace and mercy on those children of God, who openly and intentionally rejected God as their creator, never repented of their personal sins and never demonstrated and put into action their faith in God by converting and changing their ungodly perspective, attitude, and behavior into that of a traditional Christian, as described in great detail in the Bible, the greatest book ever written, and given to humankind and mankind as a gift from God to his created children.

When Jane's husband, Miles, tragically died from metastatic renal cell carcinoma that spread throughout his chest cavity and around his aorta, lungs, and throughout his mediastinum, Jane demonstrated the grace, mercy, and forgiveness of God, with regard to how she respected her husband despite that fact that her husband had betrayed her during a short-term affair with another woman, as delineated previously. Jane, being the Godly, forgiving, kind, "wonder woman-like" strong and mighty champion of (and simultaneously a pilgrim on a journey to her reunion with), God during her life on Earth and for eternity, was one of the most outstanding examples of a female version of Jesus Christ that this Earth was ever blessed with for the duration of her angelic life. Jane was indeed a gift from God and a blessing to all those human beings who were in receipt of her constant outflow of wise and Godly mentoring, good judgment, compassion, grace, mercy, kindness, physical and spiritual extraordinary beauty, patience, and inner strength to deal with, adjust to, and then overcome betrayal, treachery, abandonment, abuse (verbal, physical, social, mental, familial), and Godly inner strength and resilience to keep her eyes on the prize of her ultimate goal of never betraying her marital vows and commitment to and faith in God, during Mt. Everest ascent, journey, and pilgrimage to eternity and reunion with God, the creator of this Jesus-like angelic female, and faithful sister to Ruth, a blessing and source of encouragement to Jane throughout her trials and tribulations in dealing with her husband and children's testing of Jane's commitment to God, despite her family members' lack of appreciation and support for Jane throughout her remarkable, Godly life!

God is good. God is just. God is intolerant of truly evil and deceitful sons and daughters that he allowed to be created and born into this world and onto this Earth.

After Jane and Ruth's son got together on multiple occasions and discussed, planned, successfully organized, and accomplished finally, with success, after numerous failed attempts, the rehabilitation (alcohol, tobacco, and drug dependence) of Jane's youngest daughter and son, who both lost their marriages to divorce as a result of their alcohol or drug dependence or both, and who were both on the edge of death just before their final (God blessed), consent and agreement to enter their respective last attempts at drug and alcohol dependence rehabilitation, Jane's husband then died of metastatic cancer. Reasonable, rational, and respectful followers and believers in God's goodness, grace, mercy, and forgiveness of human sins and shortcomings would assume, expect, or conclude that Jane's two alcohol and drug-dependent youngest children would be forever grateful for their mother and cousin's stressful but persistent and resilient efforts to save their lives from drug and alcohol destruction. However, this was not the case at all. Instead, all of Jane's children failed to learn and replicate the love, grace, mercy, forgiveness, generosity, and kindness that only a God-blessed angelic woman and mentor like Jane, as it turns out, could provide for her family before her physical earthly death, and the commencement of her eternal physical and spiritual life with God, after having completed her adventure alongside her loving sister, Ruth, known as "Two Sisters, The Dynamic Due, Pilgrimage To Eternity."

Jane organized a magnificent and praiseworthy funeral service for the one man she had committed her entire life and marriage vows to, aside from God, of course, went to great efforts to generate lovely large portraits and pictures of her loving, though not perfect (no human is perfect, as we all know), husband and lifelong friend and partner during Jane's pilgrimage to eternity. Jane financed the entire memorial service and celebration of her husband, Miles, fantastic life! Despite very little to no support from her children, Jane gathered every friend, colleague, and family member who had known Jane and Miles, throughout their life journey together, and more importantly, worked diligently and fervently to both motivate, inspire, and ensure that everyone on this planet who knew and appreciated the many good and Godly deeds this married couple accomplished in their lives, would travel to, attend in person, and if they desired to, speak in honor of Miles, to celebrate (not denigrate) his many notable life accomplishments and successes!

Once again, Jane's children disappointed and frustrated her and her recently deceased husband, Miles. By either choosing not to speak about and praise their father or, in the cast of Jane and Miles' youngest son, to actually denigrate his father, Miles, in the speech he made at Miles's memorial or funeral service, Jane, Ruth, and Ruth's son were all equally surprised, saddened, disappointed, and frustrated. Not only did Jane's children not support, financially or organizationally, this worthy gathering to celebrate the life of their father, but they then, in essence, silently and subtly backstabbed their father, as evidenced by their silence or effort to disparage their father.

Years later, the above paragraph and described situation or scenario was repeated, in almost, sadly, an identical fashion, when Jane's most Godly yet most tortured (by his "prima donna former Ms. California wife," a self-declared and proven, based on her entire life behavior, narcissistic and selfish misanthrope and terrible mother and anti-mentor of all her children due to her lack of any Godly perspectives, attitudes, or values from birth until her descent in hell for her final sun tan booth session), son, Tim, was shockingly diagnosed with a very rare form of cancer that, at the time of his diagnosis, had a poor prognosis for survival after surgical or medical treatment of this form of cancer due to the location and complexity of this specific diagnosis. Tim was a pillar of faith in God to and for his family. He was always a leader with wise and sound judgment, a hard worker, and the financial guru and greatest supporter of all his family members in their time of desperation. Different times of desperation occurred for all Tim's siblings, at which point, they could always count on and rely on help being given to them, often against their own wishes ironically, by either Tim, Jane, or both Tim and Jane, to traverse the deep, otherwise drowning waters of their turbulent hurricane storms, known otherwise as their respective times of desperation. These truths can be illustrated through the telling of myriad true stories, yet only a select few will make the greatest case for the explanation of how "Holy and Angelic" Jane was, and how Jesus-like, tolerant, patient, and persevering of great and prolonged torture (similar to the character of a book in the Bible entitled "Job"), Tim was during their family years of supporting their less fortunate, less wise, less grateful and thankful (inappropriate in every sense), siblings who encountered their own harsh storms in life, often self-imposed, as a result of their lack of faith and trust in God, and ungodly perspectives, attitudes, and actions which, in most, if not all, cases, resulted in extremely difficult or even disastrous life outcomes that, luckily, God mended by utilizing his Godly servants and followers, Jane, Tim, Ruth, and Ruth's children, to improve the lives of and encourage cessation of ungodly practices (e.g., drug and alcohol abuse), and encourage the embracement of God as their savior, repenting of their sins, and turning their life one hundred and eighty degrees (in the opposite direction they had been traveling), back to God, their forgiver, savior from their early life sins, and creator, who greatly loved, respected, and wished to be reunited with them in heaven, after they accepted Jesus Christ as their savior and started to live and act as a Christian, as taught and described in the Bible, the greatest book ever written.

One such example occurred when Tim's sister (the older of his two sisters), experienced financial difficulties after having bought a very large house with her husband, who was then fired from his job and unable to find an equivalent paying job for approximately four to five years! Neither Jane nor Tim were obligated to support Lena and her unemployed husband for these five years, and Jane and Tim did not criticize them for overspending on the large home they purchased that they could now not afford the mortgage payments, especially since Lena never worked after getting married and subsequently having three children with her husband. By their Godly generosity alone, Jane and Tim volunteered to donate and support them financially so Lena and her husband would not have to declare bankruptcy as a couple and lose their home.

Jane and Tim were never appropriately loved or thanked for this "bailout" of their sister and her husband, during Jane and Tim's lifetime, or even at their memorial services, which was indeed a sad and very disappointing outcome.

Furthermore, as previously alluded to, Lena and her younger sister conspired with Tim's evil wife, after Tim's death, and before Tim's memorial service (which Lena, her sister, and Tim's wife spent not a penny on in paying for either the memorial service or Tim's burial fees and expenses, which, sadly, had to be paid entirely by Tim's Angelic and Godly mother, Jane. After Tim's memorial service had concluded, his Satanic wife had a premeditated plan which she enacted to steal all Tim's collector edition classic and custom sports cars (classic and valuable sports cars refurbishing had been one of Tim's hobbies in life), and distribute them to herself and Tim's sisters, who conspired with her in this evil act of treachery, without any payment being made to Jane, Tim's mother, for the costs of her husband's memorial service. Jane cried and lamented this truth when telling this to her loving nephew, who had assisted her in getting both her kids to agree to enter drug and alcohol dependence rehabilitation programs, which, after initial failures and multiple relapses, eventually was successful and saved the lives of two of Jane's children, who were now being given (by Tim's embezzling and evil wife who paid nothing in expenses incurred for her very own husband's funeral that she, herself, should have financed or paid for in its entirety and organized herself, rather than refusing to do this and thereby obligating and stressing out Tim's mother to perform both these responsibilities herself and on her very own), Tim's valuable collector edition sports cars to profit from, yet these same children contributed no financial support to their older brother Tim, via financially paying for his memorial service so that Tim's mother would not have to take on this entire organizational responsibility and stress in organizing his funeral and paying for the entire cost of Tim's lovely and well-organized memorial service. Again, yet another example of Jane's Godly love for her children despite being stabbed not only in the back by her evil daughter-in-law and ungrateful children, but this time, also being stabbed in her Godly heart and soul.

Several years later, Jane inherited the home of one of her elder and dear friends and neighbors because Jane, for many years, lovingly took care of this woman. Jane delivered food to her from the grocery store and took her to her doctor's appointments for many years before this woman's eventual death. Lena then asked her mother, Jane, if Lena's daughter (granddaughter of Jane) could move into this home (Lena also requested [more accurately demanded] that Jane finance a renovation of the home before Lena's daughter would move into the home, as selfish and disgusting as this may sound and actually is, in reality), after Lena's daughter had just recently been married and was starting a family of her own. Lena's daughter and her spouse/husband were allowed to move in, but after several months, suddenly stopped making rent payments to Jane. Jane confided to her nephew that she was severely disappointed and deep distressed by this behavior of her family members, which she again vented to and with her loving and beloved sister Ruth and Ruth's children, which also depressed and disappointed Ruth's family to hear of such neglect, disrespect, negligence, and irresponsible behavior and nonfulfillment of promises, and obligations that were due to and agreed to be fulfilled for and to Jane, who had spent a great deal of money to renovate that home that her granddaughter moved into eventually, and agreed to pay monthly rent for, then betrayed her grandmother and coerced Lena to consent to, both conspiring to dishonor and steal money due to her grandmother (Lena's mother, Jane).

Jane's oldest son, Tim, may have married the worst woman (or "anti-Christ wife"), ever. Her only claim to fame was being former Ms. California, but if the judges had reviewed a resume of her integrity, character, and measurements of dishonesty, selfishness, and misanthropic perspectives, attitudes, and actions toward all other human beings in her life, this woman would have been disqualified and expelled from the contest, and ceremony in the first round of, or perhaps thirty seconds after the review of her resume of "anti-Christ [future] wife" negative potential and performance.

Tim's wife, Delilah, was and is genuinely an evildoer and evil spirit. She blessed and was a simultaneous supporter and accomplice in allowing her oldest and first daughter from a previous marriage (ending in divorce, not a surprise at all for any husband to immediately recognize the "antichrist" she was and is), to move to northern California after attending university in Scotland, and live with and have a baby, out of wedlock, with a still-married man that she had an affair with. Sinister Delilah's oldest daughter was a rotten apple who fell not far from the tree but rather onto the rotting root of the poisonous apple tree, owned by the serpent, also known as Satan!

Delilah also, throughout her marriage years (many, sadly, and unfortunately for Tim, who was a Godly and devout Christian who was unwilling to dishonor his marriage vows to either his evil "fasad" and "prima donna" wife or to his loving and Holy God, both to whom he pledged his marriage vows), engaged in the nefarious and sinister practice of traveling often to the homes of her wealthy family members, at all times, sucking money (which she never deserved or merited) and the life out of her wealthy relatives, all in order to live an exotic, unwarranted, and debt-accumulating life, which she otherwise would and should not have been able to afford due to her "lazy nonwork ethic, "prima donna (fasad)," and mythical belief that she should not have to work to earn a living and support her entire family (versus only her oldest daughter, who was the only daughter she ever took with her on arrogant, exotic, and expensive trips to Europe and other exotic locations throughout the world, multiple times, again, always only with her oldest and most unethical spoiled daughter from her first marriage). She never took her husband and two youngest daughters on trips with her. Meanwhile, her Godly, Tim, despite his wife's verbally abusive nature, behavior, and actions, was a faithful husband and Godly mentor for all his three daughters (one stepdaughter and two birth daughters). He continued to faithfully and diligently perform his duties and work at their Church, where he would also take his daughters every Sunday while they were growing up at home, until they went away to college.

In just under sixty years of family gatherings, whether it be weddings, funerals, or just happy holidays, Delilah's attendance or (non) meaningful interactions and participation as a family member at these events and family gatherings was approximately five percent of these gatherings or less. God blessed all Tim's children, more so the younger two daughters than the older daughter, as previously mentioned, purely and exclusively based on the "pillar of Godly faith" that Tim was to his Godly mother, his father (imperfect but good and caring overall), his siblings, and his children, all of whom had been dependent on him throughout their lives. Tim always provided Godly advice, guidance, mentoring, and financial assistance (whenever possible and desperately needed by any of his family members) to his family, yet was never appropriately thanked or appreciated for being the Godly, responsible son, sibling, and father that Tim was to all his family members.

Whenever Ruth's children needed assistance, support, or help in any way or manner, it was always Jane and her husband, Miles, who were there for them, encouraging them, inspiring them and motivating them to both do their best and be the best possible Godly children and adults they could be. Never did Ruth's children receive any significant support or encouragement, at least that they can recall, from their uncles, aunts, or cousins, e.g., the children of Jane, Judas, and (God-doubting and disbelieving) Thomas. These uncles, aunts, and cousins all either pretended to be Godly and Christians, except for Tim, who actually was an authentic Christian, or outright rejected, declined, or neglected to live a Christian and Godly life or attend church each week, and they all suffered unnecessary anguish in their lives as a result of their rejection of God's freely offered faith, repentance of their sins, forgiveness, and acceptance of Jesus Christ as their savior, as their successful redemption from their sinful life and pilgrimage to eternity, all that was demonstrated directly to them by their mother, Jane, and maternal aunt, Ruth, during their life paths and "Two Sisters, The Dynamic Duo, Pilgrimage To Eternity."

To summarize the lifelong betrayal of Jane and Ruth by their spouses, cousins, and other family members, every instance of betrayal was stressful, hurtful, unkind, and disappointing to Jane and Ruth, yet both sisters always and steadfastly remained true and faithful to their spouses and God, regardless of the harm, insults, and injuries they seemed to have been destined by God to be tested by, and withstand with resilience and resolve to march on, straight ahead, on their "straight and narrow pathway," a trail created and designed by Jesus Christ, their savior, and redeemer, who walked the same path alongside them and completed the same pilgrimage to eternity in them and with them at all times!

After purposely abandoning their sister, whom they supposedly had come to help clean up her home (with every room filled with trash, no running water, no electricity, and thus Ruth's inability to live a healthy life in this public health nightmare cluttered and filthy home). After this act of betrayal toward their sister Ruth, Ruth's twin brother, Judas, and her youngest atheist, drug and alcohol-abusing brother, Thomas, had one last fatal or mortal sin to commit, concomitantly on both their sister, Ruth, and upon Ruth's son, who wisely and correctly knew, recommended, and begged them for help and support of his mother, to move her to a senior living community so that she could thrive and maintain whatever mental health she had left, for (what Ruth's son hoped would be many) years into the future!

Instead, Judas and Thomas conspired and agreed in secret to leave Ruth in the home that she had already demonstrated and proven repeatedly in the last ten years that she could no longer successfully manage, maintain, and pay the necessary bills to maintain the home with complete functionality necessary to maintain her own physical and mental health, e.g., properly and repeatedly pay the water bill, any necessary plumbing bills, telephone service bills, electricity bill, garbage disposal bill, and clean the home weekly to assure a healthy home and living environment. Judas and Thomas deliberately agreed on the evil plan to let their sister's mind become totally rotten with dementia, accomplished most rapidly and efficiently in their mind by leaving Ruth alone in a totally empty house, which is exactly what they did when they departed Ruth's house that week (knowing Ruth would then refill the house with trash and continue not paying all her house bills, taxes, and other expenses). Judas and Thomas not only wholly ignored Ruth's son's strong, wise (and, in retrospect, totally correct), recommendation to move Ruth out of the home that obviously (verified by a county health official who inspected the house and condemned it as unsafe to live in until it was sufficiently cleaned up, water, electricity, refrigerators, toilets, kitchen and bathroom sinks were restored to functional status and after extensive plumbing work had been completed, and even changes to the backyard were necessary to meet the requirement for a return of anyone to live in this home declared as a public health hazard! Ruth could not maintain or take care of this home, and this was clear to Ruth's son, Judas, Thomas, and the county health inspector. Despite all these facts, Judas and Thomas decided to let their sister stress out and die, one day at a time, by leaving her alone in this house for the next seven years, and their goal of ensuring her mind became a rotten tomato was achieved, and her dementia rapidly progressed in those next "seven years of hell," as Ruth later explained and revealed to her son, after Ruth finally realized that her brothers betrayed her and embezzled several hundred thousand dollars from her over the next 10 years after they sold Ruth's house for an unreasonable lower price than the home was worth and then distributed the money to covert, hidden investment accounts of Thomas and his family, and Thomas sent checks and funded his traitor (to Ruth) brother, Judas, one or more checks for thousands of dollars that Judas neither earned nor deserved, after volunteering to help and assist his sister in need, Ruth. All these embezzled "Home of Ruth" sale proceeds and checks written by Thomas to Judas were never cleared or approved by Ruth's son, who, again, was Ruth's health care power of attorney and financial power of attorney. Ruth's son, an expert in the healthcare industry, recommended the greatest and most compassionate and caring plan for his loving mother, Ruth. He suggested transitioning or moving Ruth out of her "death trap, unhealthy, unmaintainable home," and into a much more healthy environment with much less stress and less monthly payment responsibilities (which Ruth was not paying anyway in her current home, leading to the home being declared a public health hazard and condemned by the county health inspector), which would allow Ruth to experience more serenity and improved physical and mental health, or even improved physical and mental health.

Health-enhancing frequent positive socialization with other friends her age in a senior community would have improved her physical and mental those seven years that Ruth was left alone in her desolate and unclean home, instead of accomplishing the "lazy," "do nothing," "let Ruth's mind become rotten" plans that Ruth's brothers agreed upon during what turned out to be, in Ruth's very own words to her son many years later, "seven years of hell," during which her son had to repeatedly arrange treatment of multiple severe infections that Ruth experienced, all as a result of living alone without a clean and healthy living situation, often without heat or air conditioning, or running water, due to Ruth's inability or unwillingness to pay for plumbing service, telephone service, electricians, and HVAC (heating and air conditioning specialists to repair and maintain heating and air conditioning in Ruth's house. Ruth's son recommended, wisely and correctly, that Ruth's brain health and physical health would be greatly assisted and enhanced by a clean and socially dynamic environment where Ruth could interact and socialize with others her age every day, which again in Ruth's son's opinion (which was totally and despicably, completed ignored and rejected by Ruth's supposed loving brothers, who actually, through their sinister plan, most certainly hastened and exacerbated the decline of Ruth's mental health and premature death), would improve the quality, longevity, and overall physical and mental health of Ruth. After Ruth's son, Judas, and Thomas cleaned up Ruth's home (remember Judas and Thomas showed up three days late to the job because they decided last minute to go to a college football game in Northern California, all paid for with embezzled funds from Ruth's bank accounts), Ruth's son departed to his required professional conference out of state), at which point Judas and Thomas plotted another last minute and sinister plan to make Ruth's son a "scapegoat" for their irresponsible three days late arrival, and convinced Ruth that she should listen to them, ignore her son's plan, and the plan Judas and Thomas agreed to months earlier for this "clean up Ruth's home and move her into a senior community intervention to improve Ruth's physical and mental health trip and mission." Judas and Thomas backstabbed Ruth's son (during his absence, when he was already out of state at his professional conference, a treachery they never would have considered if he were there with them), and to make matters worse, Thomas subsequently lied, verbally and in a written report (falsified because, being the coward he was, he would only commit these acts of treachery toward Ruth's son when Ruth's son was not present to refute Thomas's lies and evil deceptions), during a dementia physician's interview who was evaluating Ruth for dementia, and Thomas then outrightly committed perjury and falsified a legal document, at that same physician's office visit, falsely claiming only Thomas and Judas cared for Ruth ("first-class ticket to hell"), and that Ruth's son had abandoned Ruth, and Thomas then signed off on the inaccurate and falsified written report of that dementia physician's evaluation of Ruth that day. Ruth's son was both the health care and financial power of attorney for his mother. However, unethical, drug and alcohol abuser and atheist Thomas, in a premeditated manner, knew that with this dementia report with negative and false information about Ruth's son (e.g., the lie stating that Ruth's son had abandoned her), he could then lie and say he was Ruth's only involved and responsibly caregiver, financial, and health care power of attorney for Ruth, then, over the next seven years, Thomas and Judas, actually and really abandoned their sibling and sister, Ruth, precisely as they falsely claimed Ruth's son had done, then proceeded to write unauthorized checks from Ruth's estate and bank accounts for the next seven years, all without the permission or approval of Ruth's actual, honest, committed, loving, Godly son, and legal financial and health care power-of-attorney. They ousted Ruth's Son from having permission to visit her at her home and deceptively convinced her that her son did not care for her when it was both her brothers who cared nothing for her and embezzled all her savings and her estate. This was all accomplished, after not moving their sister into a healthy senior living facility over the next seven years. They left their sister and her brain to rot in a filthy and unkept home without functioning water, electricity, heat, air conditioning, and knowing that Ruth was unable to pay her bills and live alone in a healthy manner. Ruth's sinister brothers' actions ensured that their sister Ruth would be alone and that her mental health and dementia would progress rapidly due to her having no visitors to her home or people to socially interact with for those "Seven Years of Hell on Earth." Judas and Thomas then returned after seven years of abandoning their sister, selling all her valuable furniture and possessions, embezzled the money, then put everything they could not immediately sell into a storage unit, and then sent the monthly storage bills to Ruth's loving son, whom they had disparaged and exiled from the love and home of his mother, Ruth. As if this travesty and act of sabotage was not enough (with regard to the destruction of the love and mental health of their sibling and sister Ruth, and assassination, figuratively, of Ruth's son who had faithfully been assisting Ruth physically, mentally, socially, and spiritually, his entire life and throughout the duration of her "Seven Years of Hell on Earth" and total neglect and abuse by her husband, siblings, and cousins), these "Dastardly Duo Brothers," or members of the brotherhood of Satan, then topped off their nefarious behavior by destroying the heart, soul, and mind of their sister, and functionally backstabbing their Godly and loving sister. They betrayed her when her mental health was failing and, thus, when she depended on their ethical help and behavior more than at any other time in her life. These "Dastardly Duo Brothers," after embezzling all the funds in her estate, then "topped off their sins" by selling her house at a considerable discount and at a below-market price level so they could just take any funds they received and be done with their sister (abandon and neglect her once again, this time until her physical death, having already embezzled all her net worth).

Incidentally, Ruth's house would have sold for twice the price her brothers sold it for, if they had sold it seven years earlier when it was paid off and not in disrepair, and because the housing market for selling a house was much better seven years earlier, than when the house was sold later by her sinister brothers in a depressed housing market. Her brothers hid all the money and proceeds from the sale of Ruth's house in the bank and investment accounts of Thomas, and then Thomas wrote checks from these accounts to transfer, criminally, this money to his conspiring, evil brother, Judas, who, along with his brother, Thomas, were that greatest curses in Ruth's life. Ruth's son found checks written from Ruth's estate and banking accounts, up to just under $5,000.00, signed by Thomas, unauthorized or approved, or consented to by Ruth's legal, notarized health care and financial power-of-attorney son. Only approximately twenty thousand dollars was transferred to Ruth's bank accounts after the sale of her home for several hundred thousand dollars in order to pay extremely high memory facility monthly payments for Ruth. The remainder of the money from Ruth's home sale was hidden in Thomas's investment accounts, then distributed to Thomas's wife and children upon his untimely and premature death, likely God's direct and overt message to Thomas that sinners cannot and will not escape from God's consequences, retribution, and punishment for their sins.

Despite Ruth and her two sons having their inheritance from their paternal grandparents, as instructed in their will, which was communicated to Ruth, Ruth's husband, and Ruth's children, just before their paternal grandparents' deaths, stolen and embezzled by Ruth's husband (who completely ignored his parents' "will" (inheritance instructions for their estate and possessions) instructions and never had a lawyer distribute the funds listed or abide by the instructions contained within the "will" document, which was the intent and instructions of his parents and in their "will," to those listed to receive an inheritance when they both had passed away or were deceased), and despite Ruth's children having their mother's inheritance, total net worth stolen and embezzled by her two siblings, the "Dastardly Duo Brothers," who also stole and embezzled their sister's physical and mental health by leaving her abandoned and alone in her home, which they knew very well she could not maintain on her own, for seven years, waiting for mental health to crumble, so they could then drain all her financial accounts, and sell her home, profiting from the home sale embezzled funds, which they then hid in various investment accounts and distributed to their own wives, children, and other family members, Ruth's two sons, who were never and will not, until their own deaths, be materialistic and greedy for other people's money. Ruth's two sons remained loving, trustworthy, supportive, and forever faithful to their mother, Ruth, and their maternal aunt, Jane, during these two women's "Two Sisters, The Dynamic Duo, Pilgrimage to Eternity."

Ruth's children, who made themselves available despite their otherwise busy school and work schedules, attended mutiple high school reunions with their mother, Ruth, and her older, loving sister, Jane, in Claremont, New Hampshire, at Stevens High School, one of the longest (if not the number one longest), active, continuous, yearly high school reunion programs in the United States! Ruth's children were the only children who accompanied these two angelic women as they aged significantly and gracefully, attending their 45th and 50th reunions. Ruth's children assisted them and enabled them to meet with all their supportive and loving, lifelong friends and classmates, whom they shared so many priceless and fond memories of their youth, during both their grammar school and high school years, during which God was transforming them from typical young children into selfless, unselfish, generous, kind, loving, forgiving, inspiring, motivating, angelic messengers and mothers, guided and directed by God, their creator!

During the final three years of the lives of "Two Sisters, The Dynamic Duo, Pilgrimage to Eternity," with the exception of Ruth's two sons, who remained loving, supportive, and appreciative of these two Angels' impact in and on their lives and visited both sisters as often and frequently as was possible without being fired from their jobs, were essentially abandoned, and relegated to "nonliving status," by the vast majority of their family members, including their siblings, nephews, nieces, cousins, and other family members and "friends," sadly as that may sound, and was, in reality. During these final three years of these Angels' earthly existence and just before their embarking on their continuing, even more exciting, satisfying, rewarding, appreciated, fulfilling, and universe-loving future pilgrimages to eternity, Ruth's sons frequently called both Angels, very frequently, several times per week, when they could not visit them and speak with them in person. This was an enormous, tremendous, supportive, loving, and treasured experience for all individuals involved in the calls. Jane, Ruth, and Ruth's children had all been and will be, forever, soulmates throughout their lives on Earth, physically, emotionally, socially, and spiritually, and, based on their undying, undefeatable, and everlasting love and respect for each other, will continue to be soulmates in heaven together in perpetuity.

For example, Jane, Ruth's elder loving sister and sibling, amazingly, faithfully, and sacrificially attended every single marked and significant life event in the lives of both Ruth's children, her two loving and supportive nephews! Jane deserves so much respect and admiration for her Godly caring, considerate, loving, and unmatched supportive perspective, attitude, and mentoring of her two eternally respecting and loving nephews, the sons of her younger sister Ruth! Jane attended in person, not just in sentiment, both her nephews' grammar school graduations, which were one year apart, when both her nephews graduated at the top of their respective grammar school graduation classes. Jane then attended both of her nephews' high school graduations, again one year apart, when both nephews graduated as valedictorians, All-Americans, and with many other various awards and accolades from their respective high school classes, including delivering speeches to their high school classmates and audiences at their distinct graduation ceremonies, again one year apart.

In each instance, Jane was immeasurably devoted, loving, faithful, and supportive, even ironing the graduation shirts, pants (suits), worn by each nephew immediately before they departed to their respective graduation ceremonies to deliver their written and memorized valedictorian speeches meant to motivate, energize, and inspire all their classmates and the entire audience, at their respective and separate graduation ceremonies.

The greatest joy in the lives of Ruth's two boys while growing up, during holidays, was, whenever invited and whenever possible, to drive six hours South of their hometown in order to visit their loving aunt and cousins in Southern California. Jane (even though not having enough bedrooms in her home to ensure an assigned bed for all of her siblings and their children and to all her cousins that she invited to her home for all said holiday family gatherings, e.g., during Thanksgiving, Christmas, Memorial Day, Labor Day, Presidents Holidays, and other special family gatherings to celebrate family members' weddings or funerals) would always, and without exception, be a loving, kind, gracious, generous host, ensuring that all attendees to their beloved family gatherings in her home were provided with sleeping bags and sleep pads to sleep on the living room floor (mainly for the youngest children, at the largest and most-packed house family holiday gatherings, when their parents wished to not stay in nearby hotels), and always ensured all family gatherings were always magical, thrilling, fun, exciting, Godly, and loving gatherings for all family members who attended these spectacular and fantastic family-bonding, spellbinding gatherings. All attendees at these spellbinding and thrilling gatherings always departed these fabulous events with genuine and authentic realization and a sense of family love and unity, and all these gatherings were truly motivating, inspiring, and loving gifts from God! Unfortunately, after Jane's and Ruth's deaths, the unifying and loving, generous forces of nature and God that Jane and Ruth were and are, eternally, and their loving, caring, unifying influence and impact on all their immediate and extended family members astonishingly and instantly vanished, like what one would expect in a magic show, but this occurrence was, unfortunately, a disheartening, real-life decimating "Gestalt" and "Paradigm-shifting experience and occurrence," and generated tears of regret in all their family members who had discounted, ignored, neglected, and not properly valued and cared for both these loving and angelic sisters. Their entire families instantly and forever thereafter, were left with the enormous spiritual and Godly vacuum which had now been emptied by these two sisters' earthly deaths. These two sisters' Godly love and care for their entire families had always filled the vacuum in all their family members' hearts and souls, and after their deaths, the vacuum was empty and had to be refilled with God's love "for and to them who had ears to hear (Keith Green's song and album of this similar phrase comes to mind) God's message and intent for their lives." Thereafter, these two angelic sisters' entire families had to face and confront the ultimate, final, and stark realization that God's influence in all their lives had been greatly reduced or, in some cases eliminated entirely (in the case of the atheists members of their families who either openly professed their allegiance to Satan and atheism or covertly did so by their attitudes or actions of betrayal, treachery, embezzlement, stealing inheritances, ignoring instructions in legal documents such as death wills, neglect, abandonment, or disrespect for their spouses or other fellow family members. The losses that these irreverent and ungodly family members experienced forever thereafter, and which impacted them immediately upon the deaths and completion of funeral ceremonies (even these funeral ceremonies, which were used by some of their siblings as further disgusting and dishonorable insults to and weapons against these two angels' loving relatives, e.g., siblings who were neither informed nor invited by their "family members" to the burial and memorial services of Jane in Claremont, New Hampshire when she was buried in the same grave plot with her imperfect but loving husband), seems, from a positive outlook and Godly perspective, to somehow have been a message and teaching from God to all these family members, that they should be more cognizant and enlightened in the future, to not only recognized angels sent from God to bless their lives, but also the valuable lesson and teaching that when family members mistreat, neglect, abandon, disrespect, or insult God's angels sent into their lives, that God's just response will be and always has been to deliver divine judgment upon them and accountability for their sins, often with dire consequences for these ungodly actions of ungodly family members.

Despite all these occurrences in the lives of Jane and Ruth, the take away from this true story is not ephemeral, but eternal. The message is enlightening and simple. During their adventures, known as "Two Sisters, The Dynamic Duo, Pilgrimage to Eternity," these two loving, supportive, and Godly, angelic sisters, raised by their similarly loving, supportive, and Godly parents, their father Alex, and their mother Sharon were raised stupendously by their parents, were exceptional listeners and learners, were outstandingly kind, respectful, generous, graceful, merciful, empathetic human beings and, thankfully, fabulous mothers and mentors to all their children and fellow families members, some of whom benefitted from their Godly wisdom, enlightenment, and teachings, and many who ignored, disregarded, and disrespected their Godly mentoring and life examples, much like the life of Jesus Christ, God's son, who was and always will be the ultimate life example for humans to be blessed, forgiven of their sins, redeemed, and accepted into heaven if they follow and emulate the teachings and mentoring of Jesus Christ, their God and Savior, as delineated in the greatest book ever written, the Bible!

In an effort to and in tribute to honor and characterize the trials and tribulations that both outstanding sisters endured and acknowledge their keen, successful, and God-guided navigation through the many hurricane storms they encountered in their life journeys through rough seas and to reach their final destinations, the paragraphs below, selected from both non-Bible authors and origins, and from Bible scriptures, were thoughtfully and introspectively chosen by Jane's nephews and Ruth's two sons, which they believe most characterize their ever-important impact on this world and all their friends and family members.

> "'As surely as I live,' says the Lord, 'every knee will bow before me; every tongue will acknowledge God.'" [b]

- **12** So then, each of us will give an account of ourselves to God.

- **13** Therefore let us stop passing judgment on one another. Instead, make up your mind not to put any stumbling block or obstacle in the way of a brother or sister.

- **14** I am convinced, being fully persuaded in the Lord Jesus, that nothing is unclean in itself. But if anyone regards something as unclean, then for that person, it is unclean.

- **15** If your brother or sister is distressed because of what you eat, you are no longer acting in love. Do not by your eating destroy someone for whom Christ died.

- **16** Therefore do not let what you know is good be spoken of as evil.

- **17** For the kingdom of God is not a matter of eating and drinking, but of righteousness, peace, and joy in the Holy Spirit,

- **18** because anyone who serves Christ in this way is pleasing to God and receives human approval.

- **19** Let us, therefore, make every effort to do what leads to peace and to mutual edification.

- **20** Do not destroy the work of God for the sake of food. All food is clean, but it is wrong for a person to eat anything that causes someone else to stumble.

- **21** It is better not to eat meat or drink wine or to do anything else that will cause your brother or sister to fall.

THE BIBLE, NEW INTERNATIONAL VERSION

James 4:11

- **11** Brothers and sisters, do not slander one another. Anyone who speaks against a brother or sister [a] or judges them speaks against the law and judges it. When you judge the law, you are not keeping it, but sitting in judgment on it.

Hebrews 13:1

- **13** Keep on loving one another as brothers and sisters.

1 Peter 3:8

- **8** Finally, all of you, be like-minded, be sympathetic, love one another, and be compassionate and humble.

Psalm 133

- **1** How good and pleasant it is when God's people live together in unity!

Romans 12:10

- **10** Be devoted to one another in love. Honor one another above yourselves.

Matthew 18:15

- **15** "If your brother or sister sins, go and point out their fault, just between the two of you. If they listen to you, you have won them over.

1 Corinthians 7:15

- **15** But if the unbeliever leaves, let it be so. The brother or the sister is not bound in such circumstances; God has called us to live in peace.

Ruth 1:16-17

- **16** But Ruth replied, "Don't urge me to leave you or to turn back from you. Where you go I will go, and where you stay I will stay. Your people will be my people and your God my God.

- **17** Where you die I will die, and there I will be buried. May the Lord deal with me, be it ever so severely, if even death separates you and me."

Proverbs 3:17

- **17** Her ways are pleasant ways, and all her paths are peace.

Proverbs 31:30

- **30** Charm is deceptive, and beauty is fleeting; but a woman who fears the Lord is to be praised.

1 Corinthians 15:10

- **10** But by the grace of God I am what I am, and his grace to me was not without effect. No, I worked harder than all of them—yet not I, but the grace of God that was with me.

Proverbs 31:20-21

- **20** She opens her arms to the poor and extends her hands to the needy.

- **21** When it snows, she has no fear for her household; for all of them are clothed in scarlet warm clothes.

Joshua 1:9

- **9** Have I not commanded you? Be strong and courageous. Do not be afraid; do not be discouraged, for the Lord your God will be with you wherever you go."

1 Peter 3:3-4

- **3** Your beauty should not come from outward adornment, such as elaborate hairstyles and the wearing of gold jewelry or fine clothes.

- **4** Rather, it should be that of your inner self, the unfading beauty of a gentle and quiet spirit, which is of great worth in God's sight.

1 Timothy 3:11

- **11** In the same way, the women [a] are to be worthy of respect, not malicious talkers, but temperate and trustworthy in everything.

Proverbs 31:26

- **26** She speaks with wisdom, and faithful instruction is on her tongue.

Proverbs 14:1

- **14** The wise woman builds her house, but with her own hands the foolish one tears hers down.

Deuteronomy 31:6

- **6** Be strong and courageous. Do not be afraid or terrified because of them, for the Lord your God goes with you; he will never leave you nor forsake you."

Isaiah 40:31

- **31** but those who hope in the Lord will renew their strength. They will soar on wings like eagles; they will run and not grow weary, they will walk and not be faint.

Philippians 4:6

- **6** Do not be anxious about anything, but in every situation, by prayer and petition, with thanksgiving, present your requests to God.

Psalm 139:14

- **14** I praise you because I am fearfully and wonderfully made; your works are wonderful, I know that full well.

Romans 12: 10-12

- **10** Be devoted to one another in love. Honor one another above yourselves. 11 Never be lacking in zeal, but keep your spiritual fervor, serving the Lord. 12 Be joyful in hope, patient in affliction, faithful in prayer.

Proverbs 3:17-19

- **17** Her ways are pleasant ways, and all her paths are peace.

- **18** She is a tree of life to those who take hold of her; those who hold her fast will be blessed.

- **19** By wisdom the Lord laid the earth's foundations, by understanding he set the heavens in place;

Proverbs 21:21

- **21** Whoever pursues righteousness and love finds life, prosperity, and honor.

James 1:19

- **19** My dear brothers and sisters, take note of this: Everyone should be quick to listen, slow to speak, and slow to become angry.

Romans 8:18

- **18** I consider that our present sufferings are not worth comparing with the glory that will be revealed in us.

Colossians 3:12

- **12** Therefore, as God's chosen people, holy and dearly loved, clothe yourselves with compassion, kindness, humility, gentleness, and patience.

Mark 12:30-31

- **30** Love the Lord your God with all your heart and with all your soul and with all your mind and with all your strength.'

- **31** The second is this:'Love your neighbor as yourself.' There is no commandment greater than these."

1 Timothy 5:8

- **8** Anyone who does not provide for their relatives, and especially for their own household, has denied the faith and is worse than an unbeliever.

Romans 8:11

- **11** And if the Spirit of him who raised Jesus from the dead is living in you, he who raised Christ from the dead will also give life to your mortal bodies because of his Spirit who lives in you.

CHAPTER ELEVEN

What Takeaway Life Lessons Can Be Learned And Used To Better Our Own Existence And Life Pathway And Pilgrimage To Eternity By Carefully Studying The Background, Upbringing, Perspectives, Attitudes, Motivation, Inspiration, Compassion, Empathy, Altruistic Actions And Life Philosophy, And Motherly, Angelic Behavior Of These "Dynamic Duo Sisters," As Described In The Pages Of This Book, And As Demonstrated By These "Dynamic Duo Sisters"

Throughout The Duration Of Their Existence On This Planet, Earth, Without The Reciprocity And Appreciation That Any Logical, Intelligent, And Ethical, Moral Human Being Would Expect That They Would Receive Or Should Have Received From Their Spouses And Other Fellow Relatives And Human Beings, In Return For Their Glorious, Godly, And Benevolent Behavior? In Short, These Dynamic Duo Sisters Were Only Embarking On The First Phase Of Their Pilgrimage To Eternity. Though The First Phase Of Their Journey And Adventure Was Full Of Trials And Tribulations, Undeserved And Unfortunate Lack Of Affirmation, Rewards, Appreciation, Respect, And Honor That Was Due To Them, They Were Ultimately And Divinely Rewarded, Appreciated, And Loved By Their Children And Even More So By God, Their Creator, Who Met Them At Their Pilgrimage Destination And Is Affirming, Appreciating, And Loving Them Daily For Eternity.

The Bible contains numerous examples of and perhaps the most comprehensive single source of stories of Godly women, Godly sisters, and Godly mothers, all who have, throughout history, played vital and essential roles in the providing for, protection of, and overall care and safety of their family members throughout time. One such example includes the description of Hagar, a gentile woman (a non-Israelite female), who was the first mentioned or documented woman of no particular importance or wealthy or other highly accomplished skills or status in life, to encounter an angel and subsequently describe God her Creator as "the God who sees me (or "El Roi"). The Bible has forever, and will, for eternity, provide the most precious and priceless guidance regarding how women (and men; there are no other options, as per God and the Bible), may and should aspire, endeavor, aim, and work toward the unending goal daily, weekly, monthly, and yearly to become the most God-like, kind, inspiring, motivating, graceful, merciful, empathetic, compassionate, and forgiving woman of God, which is, perhaps, contrary to popular belief in every generation, always possible, and never too late in life to commence and continue throughout one's pilgrimage to eternity, and reunion with God their creator, Heavenly Father, and most-loving family member, whose love, support, and faithfulness can and never will be exceeded or "outdone" by any living or a mortal human being on this planet Earth.

What, then, are examples of some of these select qualities, characteristics and defining features of all Godly women who seek, rightfully, to progress and perfect their Godly behavior to a level that would approach or be on par with the level of one of God's angels in heaven? Such a woman would demonstrate and manifest the following aspirations, characteristics, attitudes, traits, and actions daily:

1. Humility and Willingness to Be Taught and Learn
2. Fear of God, Obeying God's Commands
3. Faithful and Trustworthy

4. Compassionate and Kind
5. Patience and Always Forgiving
6. Frequent or Constantly Prayerful and Always Spiritually Disciplined
7. Loving and Husband-Respecting
8. Godly and Outstanding Mother, Mentor, and Homemaker
9. Generosity, Compassion, and Giving to the Poor or Less Fortunate Humans in the World
10. Possesses or Strives to Achieve and Maintain Wisdom and Discernment
11. Hardworking (Christian Work Ethic) and Diligence in all Benevolent Activities and Goals
12. Modest and Chaste

When considering the characteristics of Godly women, mothers, and sisters, what ideas and perceptions come to mind? Where would one go, or from what resource would one perform research and seek guidance from in order to learn most precisely and accurately about God's character? The answer is the Bible, which happens to be, conveniently, the answer that perfectly matches the previous question. The characteristics of God are found in both God's word, e.g., the Bible, and in His creations, otherwise known as humankind. In addition, what makes all God's children, regardless of whether they are in different phases of their lives, based on their differing ages and stages of development, from birth to death, the happiest, the healthiest, the most impactful in helping and supporting their fellow humans to achieve peace, serenity, and success in all their Godly aspirations, endeavors, ambitions, goals, and ultimately, their God-directed, God-guided, and God-enabled achievements in life? The answers to these questions and many more life-enhancing suggestions, enlightenment, and wisdom follow in the paragraphs below, which are fabulous and select excerpts/chapters from a masterpiece and classic novel entitled "Father's Eyes," written by Ruth's youngest son Winston Anselm Irons.

What makes people most fulfilled in life: parenting (mother and father combination, single mother, single father)?

Parenting experience and the manner in which parenting is delivered to children is as diverse as the stars in the sky. Is it imperative to use a rigid and single formula for best parenting to raise children in the best and most successful manner? The answer is no. This should be obvious. Many of us, including Ruth's youngest son of this book, know of or are friends or colleagues with multiple individuals with astonishingly diverse backgrounds, and in many cases, radically different upbringings and, in select circumstances, had parents who employed, successfully or unsuccessfully, shocking parental behavior and unproven or unjustified or just pure reckless and irresponsible parenting traits and failed trials. Despite these spellbinding stories and historical accounts told to us by our friends, most of these individuals (but not all) navigated the tumultuous and tempestuous storm, persevered, and were able to exit their stormy upbringing and educate and enlighten themselves, thereby effecting a metamorphosis and transformation of themselves (children in dire circumstances into adults with unlimited potential and auspicious futures) into amazingly successful, benevolent, and godly human beings! Despite the fact that there is not one formula that applies to or fits all parents and instructs them on how to properly raise their child or children, there are standard features and methods that should be known and employed to make parenting of children less stressful, more satisfying, most efficient, effective, and generate love, respect, assurance, positive self-esteem, self-confidence, and lifelong love and appreciation for God and all God-respecting family members. Christian parenting principles benefit everyone on this planet, including agnostic and atheist parents and families because they employ strategies that have been proven to be successful for thousands of years, and because when parents are mature, responsible, and wise enough to entrust the safety and well-being of their children to God and the church community, they and their children will immediately experience the relief, serenity, peace, humility, positive self-esteem, and self-confidence that results from learning godly values and principles, such as caring and loving others as much as or more than yourself, to receive God's blessings for you as parents and for your children.

All parents of any culture, religion or no religion, and from any country in the world will benefit from the true pearls of God's parenting guidelines and principles to raise healthy and happy children who are the most confident and prepared to meet all challenges in life, navigate all life's storms, and successfully contribute, in a positive way, to the betterment of society:

- Love and Honor God above all others.

- Love your children as Jesus loves you.

- Be a faithful steward.

- Do not provoke your children.

- Teach God's Word.

- Train your children to follow Jesus.

- Be humble.

- LOVE AND VALUE YOUR CHILDREN: "Fathers, do not provoke your children to anger, but bring them up in the discipline and instruction of the Lord" (Ephesians 6:4).

- POINT CHILDREN TO SCRIPTURE: "All Scripture is breathed out by God and profitable for teaching, for reproof, for correction, and for training in righteousness, that the man of God may be complete, equipped for every good work" (2 Timothy 3:16–17).

- TEACH CHILDREN THE LORD'S CHARACTER: "Come, O children, listen to me; I will teach you the fear of the Lord" (Psalm 34:11).

- PROTECT CHILDREN'S INNOCENCE: "Let no one despise you for your youth, but set the believers an example in speech, in conduct, in love, in faith, in purity." (1 Timothy 4:12).

- CHARACTER TRAINING COMES FIRST: "The fruit of the righteous is a tree of life, and whoever captures souls is wise" (Proverbs 11:30).

- TEACH TO CHILDREN'S GIFTING: "Now there are varieties of gifts, but the same Spirit; and there are varieties of service, but the same Lord; and there are varieties of activities, but it is the same God who empowers them all in everyone" (1 Corinthians 12:4–6).

- MAINTAIN PERSPECTIVE: "Woe to you, scribes and Pharisees, hypocrites! For you tithe mint and dill and cumin, and have neglected the weightier matters of the law: justice 3191 and mercy and faithfulness. These you ought to have done, without neglecting the 3192 others" (Matthew 23:23).

- PRACTICE WHAT YOU PREACH: "He did in all things as Joash his father had done" (2 Kings 14:3b).

- AN INTENTIONAL PARENTING BOOK: "That you may tell the next generation that this is God, our God forever and ever. He will guide us forever" (Psalm 48:13b–14).

- Get in God's presence.

- Make the Bible your authority.

- Lead by example.

- Set standards and keep them.

- Win their hearts.

- Become a family of sojourners (be a Christian family in this world but not of this world; live by godly standards as set forth in the Bible).

- Give presence more than presents.

- Know and honor your child.

- Prioritize unity.

HOW DO YOU RAISE A CHILD IN A GODLY WAY?

1. Lead by example.
2. Show them critical thinking skills.
3. Teach them how to love by loving them unconditionally.
4. Help them serve others.
5. Share your faith with them through scripture.
6. Pray with them.
7. Allow them to have their own faith.

HOW TO BE A GOOD PARENT ACCORDING TO THE BIBLE?

- "Discipline your children, and they will give you peace; they will bring you the delights you desire." (Proverbs 29:17). It's not irritating, aggravating, disheartening, or provoking children to anger. "Fathers, do not embitter your children, or they will become discouraged" (Colossians 3:21). How to biblically discipline your children.

- Seek your kids out, then educate and enlighten them with kindness.

- Ask good and positive questions.

- Calmly state the consequence of their action.

- Discipline with compassion.

- Be willing to make hard decisions when necessary and required.

- What makes Christian parenting different? Christian parents should be ready and willing to express love to their children. Christian parents attempt to provide their children with a tangible example of God's love for them. When people are truly loved and cared for by their parents, they get a small glimpse of what God's love for us looks like. What is the role of a godly mother to her children?

- A godly mother encourages children to seek Jesus.

- Yet you direct their attention to Jesus through it all. You show them their identities aren't in what they do but who they are in Christ. Psalm 127:3-4 says, "Behold, children are a heritage from the Lord, the fruit of the womb is a reward."

- Respect, reverence, and worship are the key ingredients to fearing the Lord.

WHAT MAKES GODLY PARENTS?

Joseph said, "With me in charge," he told her, "my master does not concern himself with anything in the house; everything he owns he has entrusted to my care. No one is greater in this house than I am." What are the biblical duties of a proper parent? Parents should teach their children the gospel. The Lord warned that if parents do not teach their children about faith, repentance, baptism, and the gift of the Holy Ghost, the sin will be upon the heads of the parents. Parents should also teach their children to pray and to obey the Lord's commandments.

WHAT DOES JESUS SAY ABOUT PARENTING?

Jesus said, "Let the little children come to me, and do not hinder them, for the kingdom of heaven belongs to such as these." What are biblical parental roles? The Bible places a strong emphasis on parents' influence as a child's initial teacher. The Bible emphasizes that parents' primary duty is to nurture and guide their children from an early age while discussing the significance of parenting in a child's upbringing (Proverbs 22:6; Deuteronomy 6:7). How should parents treat their children biblically?

Psalm 103:13: "As a father shows compassion to his children, so the Lord shows compassion to those who fear him." The good news: Fathers, nurture your children with compassion so they do not come to be afraid of you. What does God say about a disobedient child? Proverbs 29:17 has this to say to parents: "Discipline your child, and he/she will give you rest; he/she will give you delight to your heart." A Scripture, from Proverbs 13:24, reads thusly: "He who spares the rod hates his son, but he who loves him is careful to discipline him."

Does the Bible say you hate your children if you do not discipline them?

The Bible says if you love your child, you'll discipline them. And you'll do it in love and not anger. Don't buy into the idea that good parents don't discipline their children because they "love them too much." What is God's attitude towards single parenting? Single parents need to hear that they are fine, just as they are, and just as capable of raising children well as any other family. Be clear that God holds single-parent families in high regard.

Psalm 68:5 says, "A father to the fatherless, a defender of widows is God in his holy dwelling."

WHAT DOES A GODLY MOTHER LOOK LIKE?

She is confident that He will meet her physical, material, Or emotional needs. Instead of focusing on what she lacks, she speaks of God's sufficiency in her life and is grateful whether He provides much or little. A godly mother is generous. Even if she has little to share, she willingly offers it to others.

HOW TO BE A GODLY STEPMOM?

If you are a stepmom, pray and ask God to help you to love well. Ask Him to show you all of your children's hearts and how to love them better and to teach you how to pray specifically for your family.

- If you know someone who is a stepmom, pray, and ask God how you can help support your friend and her family.

WHAT IS A BIBLICAL EXAMPLE OF A GODLY MOTHER?

The most well-known mother in the Bible, Mary, conceived Jesus, the Son of God, through the Holy Spirit. She was visited by the angel Gabriel, who informed her of her unique privilege of bearing God's Son. She responded in humility, rejoicing in the Lord's greatness, and He blessed her greatly. What is the message of godly parenting? Godly parenting is to revolve the family around the centrality of God. Psalm 78:4 says, "We will not hide them from their descendants; we will tell the next generation the praiseworthy deeds of the Lord, his power, and the wonders he has done." Children are not the highest value— God is. What does healthy parenting look like?

Positive parents support a child's healthy growth and inner Spirit by being loving, supportive, firm, consistent, and involved. Such parents go beyond communicating their expectations but practice what they preach by being positive role models for their children to emulate.

WHAT ARE THE TRAITS OF A GODLY MOTHER?

These characteristics—shielding, comforting, birthing, protecting, hovering—are all godly characteristics, features, qualities, and specific examples of God-guided and God-inspired behavior and actions which are manifest in mothers because all mothers on this Earth are of Him, from Him, and by Him.

Parental responsibilities include

- providing a safe living environment;

- protecting the children from abuse and other dangers;

- paying child support as ordered;

- fulfilling the children's basic needs (food, water, shelter);

- disciplining the children;

- investing in the children's education;

- knowing the children's interests;

- protecting your child from harm.

- providing your child with food, clothing, and a place to live;

- financially supporting your child;

- providing safety, supervision and control;

- providing medical care;

- providing an education;

- making tough decisions that are not popular; if your child doesn't get angry with you at least once in a while, you're not doing your job;

- teaching your child to function independently;

- holding your child accountable;

- going along for the ride; and

- doing your best.

WHAT IS THE BIBLICAL ROLE OF A MOTHER?

Motherhood is sanctifying, but it is also sweet. Scripture teaches M others to point children toward Christ by praying for them, modeling faith and character, and training them in wisdom (Proverbs 1:8, 29:15). The role of a mother according to the Bible According to the Bible, the role of a mother is to love and care for her children. She is to teach, train, nurture, and discipline her children. A godly mother is to model holy living for her children and take care of her home. She is also to care for and help her husband. How does God want us to parent? The fundamental goal for Christian parents should be to guide their children to a saving faith in Christ and to set them on a path to maturity, bringing them to the full measure of his glory (Ephesians 4:13).

Parenting is one of God's most important callings. Children are a gift and blessing from God (Psalm 127:3–5).

HOW DO YOU CONNECT WITH PARENTAL BLESSINGS?

- You can access your parental blessings by loving your parents and appreciating them. It would be best if you did things, tangible and intangible, for them and lived a lifestyle that would make your parents proud of you. You cannot have parental blessings if the people who have parental authority over you are constantly made sad and disappointed with you due to your repeated or relentless ungodliness or irreverent behavior and actions.

- God does hold children who don't learn from their parents' mistakes accountable.

WHAT DOES THE BIBLE SAY ABOUT "PARENTS DO NOT PROVOKE YOUR CHILD?"

"And you, fathers, do not provoke your children to wrath, but bring them up in the training and admonition of the Lord" (Ephesians 6:4 NKJV).

- In Christian discipline, we bring both words and actions, warnings and consequences, into our children's situations in order to keep them on track.

HOW TO DISCIPLINE A CHILD:

- Time-Out

- Losing privileges

- Consider, only if appropriate, ignoring mild misbehavior

- Logical consequences

- Natural consequences

- Rewards for good behavior

- Praise for good behavior.

WHAT IS BIBLICAL ENCOURAGEMENT FOR SINGLE PARENTS?

- "Do not fear, for I am with you; do not be dismayed, for I am your God. I will strengthen you and help you; I will uphold you with my righteous right hand"; "A father to the fatherless, a defender of widows, is God in his holy dwelling."

- The Bible consistently asks followers to honor and love their mothers. Examples of this can be seen in Exodus 20:12, "Honor your father and your mother." and Leviticus 19:3, "Every one of you shall revere his mother and his father." What does the Bible say about a mother's love for her child? Isaiah 66:13 says, "As one whom his mother comforts, so I will comfort you." Isaiah 49:15 says, "Can a mother forget her nursing child? Can she feel no love for the child she has borne?" Proverbs 31:25 states, "She is clothed with strength and dignity; she can laugh at the days to come."

HOW DO YOU HONOR AN UNGODLY PARENT?

Here are six ways Christians can honor and show respect for ungodly parent (s):

- Forgive them. Jesus taught his disciples to pray, "Forgive us...as we forgive those who sin against us" (Mathew 6:12).

- Pray for them.

- Address them honorably.

- Be thankful for what they did (or did not do).

- Welcome them and be kind to them.

- Provide support if necessary.

WHAT IS THE HEART OF A GODLY MOTHER?

A God-fearing mom is intimately connected with God. She maintains a prayer and devotional life to keep a discerning heart. She is intentional about growing her knowledge of the truth by reading her Bible daily and committing Scripture to memory. She prays to seek God's wisdom and guidance for each day.

WHAT ARE THE CHALLENGES OF GODLY PARENTING?

Our children need love, time, guidance, discipline, and boundaries. They need to learn about values, virtues, and the importance of a strong work ethic. They need to be taught about God and the importance of prayer and be helped to value life and to love their faith. What are the four Cs of good parenting?

The four Cs are principles for parenting (care, consistency, choices, and consequences) that help satisfy children's psychological, physical, social, and intellectual needs and lay solid foundations for mental well-being.

WHAT ARE THE THREE FS OF POSITIVE PARENTING?

They are firm, fair, and friendly. These Fs emphasize the importance of being consistent with your children, setting clear boundaries and expectations, and maintaining a positive relationship with them. What are the five positive parenting skills? Being a parent comes with its share of challenges and woes. The five positive parenting skills are to be encouraging, be responsive, set the example, set boundaries, and be interactive.

WHAT ARE THE FIVE ISSUES THAT AFFECT PARENTING?

The evolution of parenting—five biggest challenges faced by parents today:

- Balancing family and career

- Being afraid to say no

- A culture of blame

- Ensuring children receive a quality education

- Overload of information

WHAT ARE THE SEVEN ROLES OF A FATHER?

Friend, encourager, teacher, leader, protector, helper, provider. What makes a good parent? Parents who make time to listen, take children's concerns seriously, provide consistent support, step back and let kids solve problems on their own (or not), and allow ample free time for play can help children thrive.

What is inadequate parenting? Neglect and neglectful parenting—neglectful parenting is a style of parenting defined by a lack of parental interest or responsiveness to a child. These parents are similar to permissive, indulgent parents in that they lack control of their children. What is the accountability of a parent? Accountable parenting means your decisions need to be explainable.

You need to be able to justify your actions and your decisions, and so do your kids. You also need to be in control of your decisions. What are the five moral responsibilities of parents? Parents need to provide shelter, food, clothes, education, and medical care to their children until they are old enough to take care of themselves. Additionally, they also need to impart emotional and social nurturing so that their children can grow up to be responsible and empathetic individuals in society.

WHAT ARE THE FIVE ROLES OF THE FATHER?

Five roles of a father you must learn to do well:

- Motivator—as a dad, you are, at times, a helper, a coach, and a friend.

- Enforcer—fatherlessness is a great concern in our society today.

- Encourager—every child loves positive fatherly encouragement.

- Trainer.

- Counselor.

WHAT ARE THE FIVE ROLES OF THE FATHER?

- Visitation and custody problems

- The effects of continuing conflict between the parents

- Less opportunity for parents and children to spend time together

- Effects of the breakup on children's school performance and peer relations

- Disruptions of extended family relationships

SEVEN PARENTING MISTAKES THAT MAY ADVERSELY AFFECT A CHILD'S MENTAL HEALTH, STRENGTH, AND FORTITUDE:

- Minimizing your kid's feelings

- Always saving (or preventing) them from experiencing failure in life

- Overindulging your kids

- Expecting perfection

- Making sure they always feel comfortable

- Not setting parent-child boundaries

- Not taking care of yourself

SIGNS OF EMOTIONALLY NEGLECTFUL PARENTS:

- Speak with a cold and unfriendly tone

- Unresponsive to the child's feelings

- Dismiss the child's emotions

- Don't talk to the child very much

- Spend little time with the child and make them feel they are unwanted

- Less positive feedback or praise

- Express less affection

HOW DOES AN ANGRY PARENT AFFECT A CHILD?

It can make them misbehave or get physically sick. Children react to angry, stressed parents by being unable to concentrate, finding it hard to play with other children, becoming quiet and fearful, rude and aggressive, or developing sleeping problems.

FIVE COMMON PARENTING STRUGGLES:

- Fear—when parents struggle with fear, it often causes them to think of the worst-case scenario.

- Anger—kids don't always listen and can drive us to the edge.

- Doubt—do you second guess everything and worry you've made the wrong choice?

- Control.

- High expectations.

WHAT ARE THREE SIGNS A CHILD IS BEING NEGLECTED?

A child's basic needs—such as food, clothing, or shelter—are not met, or they aren't properly supervised or kept safe. A parent doesn't ensure their child is given an education. A child doesn't get the nurturing and stimulation they need. This could be through ignoring, humiliating, intimidating, or isolating them.

WHAT IS THE BEST PARENTING STYLE?

The parenting style that is best for children is the supportive style. It's a style where you are warm, loving, and affectionate, but you also create structure and boundaries for your children, and you guide their behavior.

WHAT GENERATES HAPPINESS AND MAKES PEOPLE MOST FULFILLED IN LIFE?

Education. It has been said that there are perhaps four essential and basic premises and purposes for school and education of all humans: academic (intellectual), political and civic purposes, socialization, and economic purposes. People often underestimate the importance of education to happiness and fulfillment, especially regarding "nonmonetary life satisfaction," contentment, tolerance, flexibility, and kindness traits that directly result from higher education levels.

Happiness can be generated in many distinct ways and by many different means. One way that happiness is achieved is via learning and implementing, on a daily basis, pure and selfless attitudes and actions.

One definition of happiness might be described, in real-life terms, as a state of peace in which there is no upheaval, violence, excessive or extreme: anger, discouragement, depression, anxiety, fear for one's safety or future well-being, jealousy, guilt, regret, and no ill or evil attitude, intent, or hatred of or directed toward others in your life. Kind, positive, uplifting, encouraging, graceful, merciful, tolerant yet not condescending or compromising (e.g., defending and encouraging ethical and moral attitudes, communications, and actions at all times), constructive words, phrases, and communicated sentences create happier humans, and thus a more fulfilled world. When one is content with oneself, happiness is inextricably involved and also present. The relationship between education and happiness is multifaceted and complex. Education strongly correlates with future happiness.

Happiness and positive emotions create dopamine and serotonin. When these substances are released into the brain, they positively affect our memory and our brain's ability to learn. These chemicals also increase the brain's capacity to make connections and make these connections faster. Happiness comes from what we do.

Fulfillment comes from why we do it. Education may have both a direct effect on overall happiness and an indirect effect through the social and financial benefits it affords. Happiness, in this case, is defined as satisfaction with the way one's life is going.

Research suggests that the more education you have, the happier you tend to be. The effect can also be both positive and negative, or dependent on your age and position in life. Education fosters control of one's own environment, a higher level of self-esteem, and a positive perspective on the future. These three factors, in turn, affect well-being positively and could be potential mechanisms linking education and well-being.

Does the highest possible level of education that each individual may pursue and successfully complete make that individual happier? Although the answer to this question will always be open to debate, and rightly so; in general, the general consensus is and probably always will be that trade or professional school-educated and college or university-educated adults tend to live happier lives with a greater sense of fulfillment, serenity, and both a greater willingness and likelihood to be both financially and attitudinally inclined to contribute back to society in myriad positive ways.

These positive contributions, often made during mid-career or later in the career of persons possessing higher levels of education and professional expertise, may manifest in many distinct ways that eventually become apparent to the general population and the world in general. Examples of these positive contributions, again, the result of higher education levels in these individuals, include: parents being more capable of educating their children throughout their lives; instilling better judgment and decision-making skills in their kids based on their own higher education level and experiences in the world (e.g., after world studies or world travel in, during, or after college, e.g., in the midst of their career experience and work-related travel responsibilities); being able to retire at earlier ages and write novels that benefit society or become involved in charitable groups, organizations, and other societies (e.g., increased local church involvement [youth group leadership roles, deacons, elders, Bible study members or leaders], missionary trips, memberships and proactive roles in: Lion's Club, Elks Club, the Masons, Kiwanis Club, Big Brothers and Big Sisters organizations, nursing and assisted-living facilities, juvenile hall or prison ministries, national parks supporters, Greenpeace, and involvement in other local and worldwide charitable and benevolent organizations. Individuals with higher levels of education tend to exhibit greater levels of confidence, a better sense of independence, and stronger feelings of control over their lives.

Graduates of college or university-level education and training programs tend to be more resilient and less depressed.

The highest possible education level that all individuals can and should be encouraged to pursue and attain will not only benefit that individual but ultimately will benefit everyone they interact with and the society they live in and now in the age of the worldwide Internet and international news and media may instantly, powerfully, and most importantly, positively influence, motivate, and inspire individuals, societies, and countries throughout the world and universe (perhaps individuals in international space stations, the moon, or on Mars in the future)!

Education, independent of innate ability, helps spur innovation and technology, and it contributes to productivity and economic growth. A key element in this process is that education is essential to adopt the technology that produces innovation and ideally affects positive, benevolent, godly aspirations, purpose-driven life tasks and pursuits, making the world a safer, kinder, more graceful, compassionate, merciful, and better, easier place to love others and live in peace, humility, and with the greatest possible level of happiness and serenity.

Why is learning important for success? Learning new things gives us a feeling of accomplishment, which, in turn, boosts our confidence in our own capabilities; you'll also feel more ready to take on challenges and explore new business ventures. Acquiring new skills will unveil new opportunities and help you find innovative solutions to problems.

What defines fulfillment in life is and should always be open to suggestions, modifications, and improvements, but has been described in the past, seemingly accurately and concisely, as involving, amongst many other possible components and definitions, the following factors or descriptive phrases: "focus on others," "unfolded self and life," "worthwhile life," and "positive impact and legacy."

Fulfillment in life may often be rapidly realized and felt first-hand by focusing on others and how an individual or collective, organized group might bring greater ease and happiness to other human beings' lives, e.g., volunteer work or other ministries offering help, encouragement, or services to others, expecting never to be repaid and nothing in return for that which was given or performed with a generous and caring attitude, perspective, and intent.

Eight important, critical, and essential aspects or factors to realize and achieve zenith happiness and fulfillment:

1. Be with others who make you smile.

   Humans are happiest when around those who are also happy, but do not ignore or neglect those in need of help or happiness.

2. Hold on to and do not compromise your values.

3. Accept good, recognize bad, in life, and always attempt to maximize good.

4. Imagine and envision, in every life scenario, how to arrive at the best outcome.

5. Obtain the highest level of education possible, studying and completing assignments and examinations you may not enjoy, to prepare, qualify, and enable you to pursue, later in life, occupations and hobbies that you love that will positively impact the world, and that you are passionate about.

6. Seek or create godly, specific and focused, executable, achievable, purpose-driven life aspirations, attitudes, behavior, communication, occupation (s), and goals.

7. Listen, look, sense, and feel God's direction, guidance, protection, and reassurance that you were created in God's image and success is God's intention for you, and know this deep within your mind, heart, soul, and physical presence on Earth.

8. Have the highest, strictest, most demanding standards of ethics, morals, integrity, honesty, and work ethic for yourself, and thereby set and define an example of best behavior, most positive aspirations, motivations, intent, outlook, and attitude for those who know you or do not know you but are around you, to positively motivate and

inspire others to follow or emulate your life philosophy of "positive actions and attitudes" inspire and motivate other humans that you interact with more than "negative actions, attitudes, comments, and criticisms."

HOW DOES EDUCATION MAKE A DIFFERENCE IN LIFE?

Education helps people become better citizens, obtain better-paid jobs, and helps individuals better decipher the differences between good and bad intent or aspirations, attitudes, behavior, and between selfishness and selflessness. Education enlightens individuals regarding the vital importance of hard work and the need for perpetual daily continuing self-education to maximize an individual's ability to adapt to changes in life and constantly update and improve their activities and performance to achieve success in life, no matter what changes or new circumstances they are forced to confront, analyze, overcome, or improve to achieve success and efficiency in completing their short and long-term goals.

A God-focused education from birth to physical death, also may result in an auspicious, magnificent, and gracious society whereby all members have the most significant potential to live righteously and respectfully by knowing and respecting rights, laws, and regulations based on biblical teachings and values established by God, the Creator of all humans, on this Earth, in this universe (and other universes), whether certain individuals choose, adversely, to ignore or disregard this truth, or, hopefully, properly educated and enlightened individuals discover on their own or are taught by their parents, otherwise mentors, or their church communities.

HOW DOES LIFE SATISFACTION AFFECT HAPPINESS?

The relationship between life satisfaction and happiness is an important area within the field of positive psychology. The obvious and positive link between life satisfaction and happiness is hard to ignore. By definition, happiness is considered to be a short-term or day-to-day variable and essentially an emotional state or feeling, whereas the concept of "life satisfaction" in contrast, is regarded to be a more a general and long-term life perspective or goal and aspiration or mindset and is more linked to or based on critical thinking, philosophical, and cognitive processes in each individual's mind, heart, and soul.

Higher or Highest education levels that individuals should be encouraged to seek out and achieve by parents, friends, church, or other community members and mentors include (amongst many other benefits not listed here): potential and high probability of positive achievements, successes, contentment, well-being, satisfaction, fulfillment, auspicious or unlimited choices for occupations, and higher chances of job satisfaction and, in general, flourishing in life.

HOW DOES EDUCATION SAVE LIVES?

Highly educated people are much less vulnerable to health risks and are more likely to make healthier choices for themselves, their children, their family members, and hopefully share their vitally important knowledge and education with everyone in their communities. Educational attainment enables a person to experience more positive health outcomes by being able to better navigate their own health and healthcare journey through life and to make wiser and more prudent decisions related to personal health choices, behaviors, and avoiding deleterious and harmful or fatal behaviors.

Learning has been shown to help improve and maintain our well-being. It can boost self-confidence and self-esteem, help build a sense of purpose in life and foster connections with others.

It has been asserted that lower education levels are potentially or can be associated with "a lack of psychosocial resources," including less or suboptimal levels of: a sense of control, resilience, the ability to delay gratification, and less access to cultural activities, thus increasing that individual's potential exposure to more daily stress, frustration, and discouragement. Lower levels of lifelong education attainment is often associated with a lack of control and resilience, and higher stress levels. This can negatively impact a person's mental health and lead to psychiatric and psychological conditions such as anxiety, depression, or even schizophrenia or bipolar disease, and many other personality disorders and other psychiatric diagnoses.

Therefore, education can be the key to success and a better life outcome, both in a physical health sense and mental health sense. Is education more important than mental health? Your excellent grades, education, and accomplishments in life that resulted at least in part from your education will always seem to be of supreme importance. However, your mental health is and will always be more important. Luckily, the more you study, the greater your brain function and mental health may improve. What a wonderful, enlightening, and remarkable fact!

WHY DOES EDUCATION AFFECT LIFE EXPECTANCY?

The longer individuals continue to educate themselves, progressing to the highest possible level of education and expertise in one or more fields of study (e.g., master's degree or doctoral degree or higher), their life expectancy has a much greater chance of being extended to older ages, possibly due to several suggested reasons, including: higher levels of income (e.g., can afford to make healthier choices in diet such as organic vegetables and afford health and dental insurance), health or "healthier lifestyles" (higher-educated individuals are less likely to be smokers because they know smokers often die of lung cancer, chronic obstructive pulmonary disease [COPD], emphysema, head and neck cancer, heart attacks [myocardial infarctions], and strokes [cerebrovascular accidents]), better-paying, more stable jobs that may provide health insurance or lessen the premium payments required to have an excellent health insurance plan that covers preventive health interventions in addition to routine payment of unexpected medical diagnoses or accidental injuries. Longer years and duration of education in school have been proven to be associated with a statistically significant decrease in depression symptoms and complaints.

Low educational levels are associated with increased levels of both anxiety and depression. How does learning improve the brain?

Learning changes the physical structure of the brain. These structural changes alter the functional organization of the brain. Learning thus organizes and reorganizes the brain. Different parts of the brain may also be ready to learn at different times.

DOES STRESS AFFECT EDUCATION?

Not exercising while studying in school (and thus not naturally ridding stress from your body while in school) may be counterproductive to an individual's desire and wishes to be the best student and to get the best education possible. When stress is not dealt with or allowed to accumulate in the body and mind, it then can rise to overwhelming levels (school-related stress) that may then actually reduce an individual's desire and motivation to proficiently complete school work, thus negatively impacting that individual's overall academic performance, accomplishments, and achievement, or, in a worst-case scenario, potentially increase the odds of that student dropping out of school.

Stress can also cause health problems such as depression, poor sleep, substance abuse, and anxiety.

What are several common and well-known reasons that students have anxiety problems that, more often than not, may be managed successfully with regular exercise and other forms of relieving the body and mind of excessive or extraordinary stress? In some children, fear and worry associated with school anxiety is related to a specific cause, e.g., being bullied by other students or teachers or some other traumatic, disruptive, or otherwise unpleasant event at school. Other students may experience anxiety, which is more general in nature or related to social reasons, phobias, performance anxiety, or sundry other reasons.

CAN THE BRAIN CHANGE WITHOUT LEARNING?

This question can be succinctly and precisely answered by studying the importance of brain connections and synaptogenesis. Basically, connections between neurons, through synapses—especially when in an educational environment or situation such as school and during learning of new concepts and ideas every day of your life (the goal) for the remainder of your life—are constantly changing throughout all of our lives and are predominantly responsible for continuing learning and memory maintenance, sustenance, and preservation throughout your life in the brain.

WHAT MAKES PEOPLE MOST FULFILLED IN LIFE?

Diet, exercise, sleep, positive and frequent socialization, and love.

A great and quick read for all individuals, read by and memorized many years ago by Ruth's youngest son while still in school, is a book (copyright 1999, with online updated information over many years now), entitled "Living to 100, Lessons in Living to Your Maximum Potential at Any Age" by Thomas T. Perls, MD, MPH, Margery Hutter Silver, Ed.D, and John F. Lauerman.

Below is a summary or synopsis of sorts, describing the enormous and immense value and wisdom contained in the findings and descriptions in this book of the research that was done to learn every facet and idiosyncrasy of the history, background, lifestyle, health habits, issues, or substances used or avoided in life, social habits, exercise, sleep, dental hygiene (e.g., toothbrushing and dental flossing), exercise, indulgence in sinful, poisonous, toxic habits, abuses, dependencies, e.g., overuse or abuse of prescription medications, use of illicit drugs that are toxic to the brain and body [alcohol, smoking, of tobacco/marijuana/cloves/cocaine/others, chewing tobacco, excess consumption of fat, sugar, protein, or too frequent eating habits versus more healthy intermittent fasting]) and assimilated all the research they obtained from interviews, surveys, and family member histories regarding all persons worldwide that reached the age of one hundred years old or older." (Living to 100, Lessons in Living to Your Maximum Potential at Any Age by Thomas T. Perls, MD, MPH, Margery Hutter Silver, Ed.D, and John F. Lauerman, 1999) Centenarians, once a rarity, are the world's fastest-growing age group: there are currently about fifty thousand people over the age of one hundred in the United States alone, almost three times as many as there were in 1980. Centenarians are setting the gold standard for healthy aging. What can we learn from these pioneers? How can people decades younger apply the centenarians' longevity lessons to their own lives? These are the questions Harvard scientists Thomas Perls and Margery Hutter Silver set out to answer when they launched the New England Centenarian Study. As they probed beyond disease to identify the parameters of an energetic later life, Perls and Silver realized that the key to preserving health and vitality lies not in learning how people stay young but in understanding how they age well. By identifying lifestyle patterns, vitamins, and medications that contribute to aging well—and may even help slow down the aging process—they show how all of us can maximize the healthy portion of the life span. Filled with personal profiles, informational sidebars, and quizzes, Living to 100 offers inspiration and solid scientific information to the more than seventy-five million people alive today who can look forward to their ninth and tenth decades.

The importance of sleep to health, longevity, happiness, and fulfillment cannot be overstated.

Getting enough rest can help reduce stress, improve your mood, and boost your energy levels.

Unfortunately, with the busy lifestyles that many people lead, rest is often put on the back burner. This is why maximizing rest is essential for optimal health and happiness. It's no secret that sleep is an integral part of a healthy lifestyle, but getting a good night's shut-eye could also be the key to feeling contented.

HOW DOES SLEEP AFFECT THE QUALITY OF LIFE?

Sleep or lack of sleep may positively or adversely, respectively, affect nearly every tissue type, all organs, all physiologic processes, all chemical reactions, and the short-term and long-term health of and longevity of our body and physical, mental, social, and spiritual life. Sleep affects growth hormones, stress hormones, our immune system, appetite, breathing, blood pressure, and cardiovascular health. Is sleep the most important thing in life? Some might argue that the answer to this question is yes because a good night's sleep recharges humans and prepares them for optimal functioning the following day. Others might argue that sleep is the second most important thing in life, "taking a second seat or second fiddle" to the productive use of our daytime school or work hours available each day. Daily decisions are best executed with the most wisdom and discernment after a good night of restful and deep, restorative sleep. Wise decisions, choices, exercise, and other school or work activities that occupy our daytime, daylight, or night shift awake hours are most efficiently and effectively executed and consistently performed on a daily basis following restful sleep each preceding evening.

Sleep, thus, is vital to preserving the integrity and maximum health of our bodies and uninterrupted continuation of errorless myriad chemical processes, neurotransmitter functions, and other physiologic processes occurring each second in our amazing and miraculous human bodies, all created by God and created in the image of God. Sleep is essential to every process in the body, affecting our physical and mental functioning the next day, our ability to fight disease and develop immunity, and our metabolism and chronic disease risk. Sleep is truly and genuinely interdisciplinary because it touches every aspect of health.

HOW DOES SLEEP CONTRIBUTE TO HAPPINESS?

Sleep gives us more energy and improves our mood and libido. And for men, getting enough sleep is also linked to the ability to achieve and maintain an erection. Does lack of sleep affect the quality of life?

Lack of sleep or sleep deficiency is linked to many chronic health problems and increases various major and clinically significant health risks and the incidence and frequency of conditions such as heart disease, kidney disease, high blood pressure, diabetes, stroke, obesity, depression, infections, and is also linked to a higher chance of injury in adults, teens, and children. There is no 100 percent consensus on how many hours of sleep each individual needs at every stage of life, and the optimal number of sleep hours may vary considerably in different individuals and may be dependent on the activities and intensity or strenuousness of those activities of that individual on that particular day. However, in general, average healthy adults need at least seven hours (eight hours may be optimal) of sleep per night. Babies, young children, and teens need even more sleep to enable their growth and development. Other factors may complicate these simple generalizations of necessary sleep hours, where more than eight hours or less than seven hours may be preferred for various health reasons, e.g., someone who is ill and did not receive any deep and restful sleep the previous night, may require more hours of sleep, and someone who took a four-hour nap earlier that day may not require a full eight hours of sleep later that day and night to feel fully rested the next morning.

WHY IS SLEEP IMPORTANT EMOTIONALLY?

Sleep stages include stages 1. and 2 (considered light sleep, but not fully restorative and restful stages of sleep; interestingly, people who consume alcohol, caffeine [e.g., coffee or chocolate], or certain nonprescription or nonessential prescription medications [e.g., taking narcotic pain meds just before sleeping when their pain level is minimal and does not require narcotic pain medication]) that can relegate that patient to being trapped in stage 1 or 2 sleep all night, instead of being able to enter into the restful and restorative deep sleep stages known as stage 3, stage 4, and REM (rapid eye movement) stage. Sufficient deep and restful sleep, especially stage 3, stage 4, and REM sleep facilitates the brain's processing of emotional information.

During sleep, the brain works to evaluate and remember thoughts and memories, and it appears that a lack of deep stages of restful and restorative sleep is especially harmful to the consolidation of positive emotional content. In one study, which is neither all-inclusive nor proof of universal truth for every individual on the planet, studied participants who slept seven hours and six minutes rated themselves as "perfectly happy." People who slept seven hours rated themselves as "mostly happy," and those who slept for six hours and fifty-four minutes reported themselves as "somewhat happy." Take what you wish from this study's findings and results, of course, always with "a grain (or large chunk) of salt."

Having a wider set of social contacts, which leads to a greater and more significant number of satisfying relationships and faithful, positive, and supportive friends, is vitally important for happiness, longevity, and fulfillment in life.

Social interactions and relationships, positive and negative, can all be educational and contribute to an individual's valuable lessons in learning to navigate stormy waters in this world, also known as this tumultuous and tempestuous world that we live in. Relationships are indelibly connected to some of the strongest (and potentially most positive and life-invigorating, motivational, and inspirational) emotions individuals can and should experience in life. Even negative relationships, which should be avoided whenever possible (especially abusive, unethical, immoral, or other evil relationships), can make an individual more resilient in the life path they will navigate, hopefully with greater wisdom and insight that they acquired and learned from their past relationships, positive and negative.

Social connections make people happier, more content, and calmer.

Satisfying relationships are also associated with better health and greater longevity. Benefits of socialization What is socialization? And why is it important? Social interaction has been said to be a basic human need, just as food, shelter, and water have been considered to be life-sustaining basic human requirements for centuries.

Simply stated, the more socializing an individual engages in, the greater one's chances are of living longer, especially when these interactions are with great mentors.

WHAT DEFINES "GREAT MENTORS"?

Great mentors are highly educated, healthy diet-consuming, exercising, non-sexually immoral (or otherwise unethical, dishonest, selfish, or ungodly) individuals, and nonalcohol or drug-abusing individuals. These great mentors are defined by their life example and daily behavior as being reliable, honest, benevolent advisors who seek to enhance the spiritual, mental, social, and physical health of all their advisees, e.g., persons being advised by someone or their mentor (s). Human interactions are of vital importance to rapidly and most efficiently and effectively helping our brain and body experience, interpret, and then comprehensively analyze and understand what is going on around us and what events and human reactions resulted from our interaction and communications, then filing these experiences and episodes of learning, one file at a time, in mental and physical file cabinets that categorize and organize these events and define the context of each of these human interactions and consequences, helping individuals, much like a supercomputer would or like the processes of quantum computing that ultimately result in that individual being a progressively smarter, more sophisticated, and more complex quantum computer-like human with ever-increasing critical reasoning skills and problem-solving ability, agility, prowess, and expertise, with every subsequent problem encountered.

Moreover, when relationships are unexpectedly negative, disappointing, discouraging, or even devastating, and thus challenge an individual right up to the perceived limit of that individual's maximum braking point (keep in mind, however, that God, in the Bible, states that humans will never be tested beyond the limits God bestowed on his creations, e.g., humans, and that He had empowered them to withstand and overcome because of God's love for all humans.

Therefore, these adverse experiences and adverse human interactions can, ironically and counterintuitively, actually immensely and instantly help us expand and extend what were previously considered to be a personal limitation levels for handling or dealing with stressful or dire circumstances in life, facilitating persevering through that life-challenging event and ultimately expanding, dramatically, how that individual sees the world and the new near-invincible, within reason, potential they have to deal with future unexpected and surprising challenges in life.

Socialization affects an individual's stress levels in many ways. For instance, socialization increases a hormone (serotonin) that decreases anxiety levels and makes us feel more confident in our ability to cope with stressors. Socialization, by definition, requires individuals to seek out, listen to, and act on the needs of others to establish and maintain those friendships; put another way, focusing our energy outward as opposed to inward, producing a less self-centered and selfish individual and concomitantly initiating a type of metamorphosis, e.g., changing a single-colored, crawling caterpillar into a beautiful, multicolored and flying butterfly in that human.

Twenty-one ways to create, maintain, and sustain long-term connections with other individuals:

1. Smiling, as simple and effortless as that may sound and seem, is very successful and satisfying.
2. Make direct eye contact and be sincere and honest in all communications.
3. Schedule significantly long and effective meeting or gathering times for deep discussions.
4. Listen intensely, proactively, and in a fully engaged manner, which demonstrates true and genuine concern.
5. Actively show and demonstrate, not just by words but via your actions, your support, and your love.
6. Communicate sensitively, sincerely, and efficiently covering necessary topics in the time allotted.
7. Seek always to encourage, support, motivate, inspire, and reassure, demonstrating your loyalty.
8. Whenever possible, focus on helping and uplifting others above and beyond focusing on self.
9. Always strive to be authentic and real versus elite or condescending.
10. Respect other individual's boundaries.

11. Attempt always to remain focused on the present and future, more than the past.
12. Spend minimal time on meaningless, insignificant, or inconsequential topics.
13. Be equitable in listening and speaking during the conversation, as necessary.
14. Offer admiration when appropriate and discouragement of bad ideas as well.
15. Seriously interpret on a minute-to-minute basis how you make others feel.
16. Show empathy by listening to other's point of view before ever responding.
17. Listen to feelings and intentions of words spoken or written between the lines.
18. Offer and be open to receiving, when appropriate, honest, and sincere feedback.
19. Be willing, prepared, and committed to creating and nurturing relationships.
20. Have an aspiration and intent to give rather than receive most often, whenever possible.
21. Always be open to new relationships, especially those that will enhance one's health.

An essential aspect of human society is the fact that an individual's life is positively enhanced, intertwined, and inseparable (at least in regard to optimizing longevity) from, preferably, positive more than negative interactions and social relationships with other diverse individuals from all different backgrounds, cultures, and countries.

Full social participation is such a fundamental human need and desire. It has been suggested that a lack of any social connections may significantly increase an individual's odds of premature death, possibly up to or by as much as 50 percent. Social connectedness, more often than not, leads to longer life, better health, and improved well-being. One definition of social connectedness is the degree to which people have and perceive a desired number, quality, and diversity of relationships that create an overall sense of belonging to a meaningful group of other humans, and being cared for, valued, and supported by the group. Socialization prepares people to participate in social groups by teaching them the norms and expectations of those groups. Socialization three primary goals include: teaching impulse control while developing a conscience, preparing and training people to perform certain social roles, and education by cultivating shared sources of meaning and value specific to each social group.

The family has been said to be (this has been confirmed over thousands of years now) the most important agent of socialization for children. Children feel secure and loved when they have strong and positive family relationships. Positive family relationships engender a sense of security, safety, and serenity to all family members. The educational impact and lifelong value of life aspects and strategies that are tried, practiced, and proven on a daily basis in positive communicating family members are often understated or even completely ignored by some individuals, much to their detriment.

Family members in godly, church-attending, neighborhoods and communities learn to effectively and efficiently resolve conflict through attentive listening and using wisdom and sound judgment in determining right versus wrong attitudes, aspirations, and motivations of the individuals involved in each conflict. These same family members can then work as a team to prevent future unnecessary disputes or conflicts, to the best extent possible, and thereby enjoy each other's company in an immensely more satisfying manner than if proper conflict resolution is not adequately addressed or ignored altogether. Positive family relationships are built on quality time spent with all members of the family on an equitable basis to the best extent possible, communication (e.g., intense and attentive listening without talking or with minimal verbal responses until someone has finished stating their reasoning for the actions they took or the things they said), teamwork (e.g., group problem solving with all family members' input, preferences, and recommendations being honestly and seriously considered and implemented in final conflict resolutions), and appreciation of each and every family member with equal and large amounts of love being graciously or mercifully given to each family member (sometimes more deserved than other times).

Parents' values and behavior patterns profoundly influence those of their daughters and sons.

Suggested goals of socialization are many, such as self-regulation, a sense of self, motivation, cultural beliefs and morality, and both physical and mental benefits, including increased cognitive ability, good mental health, communication skills, independence, and improved physical health from infancy to centenarian! Individuals who practice and perfect peaceful, moral, ethical, and otherwise positive social relationships, in general, are known to exhibit or possess better mental health or less mental health problems, e.g., less psychological or psychiatric issues, conditions, or diagnoses.

Social activity helps an individual discover and learn, hopefully, healthier lifestyle habits such as the mind, body, and soul health benefits of more frequent and more vigorous exercise and a better diet. Staying social throughout one's life also help individuals periodically or intermittently "blow off steam" or "destress."

Socialization by individuals, learned at the earliest age possible, such as in preschool, ideally, has been demonstrated throughout time and is now commonly known to stave off feelings of loneliness, sharpen memory, hone and enhance cognitive skills, increase one's sense of happiness and well-being, improve that individual's mood, generate feelings of happiness, lower than individual's risk of dementia, with a resultant and concomitant benefit to the individual of expected or anticipated increased longevity (socialization helps you live longer)!

It has been said that people who are isolated face a 50 percent greater risk of premature death than those who have stronger and more substantial social connections. Furthermore, positive social interactions promote a sense of safety, belonging, and security and are thus highly beneficial to the development and maintenance of that individual's brain health.

Lastly, socialization enables and allows individuals to confide in others and let them confide in you, which is like an imaginary—but real in this case—super vitamin for that individual's mental health, allowing excessive positive emotions to be shared with others (benefitting all involved) and prevents the accumulation and buildup of negative emotions by allowing extreme or excessive negative emotions to be vented so that they may safely exit that individual's body and mind, and not build up in pressure and in force as that of a volcano or earthquake just before the eruption or cracks/explosions, respectively, commence, often with precarious or disastrous and perilous results and outcomes. Social support may reduce your blood pressure amidst or during stressful tasks and boost your immune system.

It has been observed and well-documented that spouses with strong social support networks had better immune system functioning than those with low support levels or fewer support networks when caring for a partner with cancer.

CHAPTER TWELVE

"Ode To Outstanding Mothers In Every City, Country, Culture, and Society Throughout The World" And "Ode to Outstanding Mothers Who Blessed World Via God's Grace Before Heaven's Eternal Life"

"An Angel sent from heaven and returned to heaven:

Daughter of loving parents and loving sister to all siblings. Christian Mother and mentor of children whose love, humility, intelligence, leadership, patience, compassion, charity, ability to lift the spirits of loved ones, friends and foes alike, and lion-like courage/resolve to confront, persevere, and "forgive the unforgivable" forever endeared you, Mother, to your sons and fellow human beings who both love and respect you and will forever cherish the positive force of nature that you are and your having left this Earth a more pleasant place as a result of your selfless devotion to others, before returning to heaven to continue miraculous and healing acts of compassion, mercy, and grace that you perfected while on earth. Priceless and immeasurably important are your wise and reverent teachings. Your unconditional love for others and exemplary altruistic life which brought joy, happiness, and inspiration to all fellow humans within your sphere of influence were and are your ongoing gift to this world. You lived your life as Jesus Christ taught in The Bible. Your Motherly nurturing passion and instincts did not go unnoticed. Selfless sacrifices, intimate listening ability, caring attitude, and proactive spiritual guidance were your strengths and immensely impacted and influenced the development and maturation of your children, who all excelled in life as a result of your Angelic Motherly Love.

God transiently gifted Mother to all her children to shape and mold their destiny, then redeemed and reunited Mother for eternity with her loving parents, family, and God/Creator in heaven. God bless your soul, Mother. The universe mourns the loss of your positive Spirit on Earth whilst heaven rejoices in your return to your glorious home.

Thanks be to God for you, Mother, and your God-inspired guidance and teachings which you so generously shared with your children. Thank you and all God's love to you Mother, for your dynamic, vital, and precious time on this Earth, the Godly mentor you have been, are, and will be forever to all your children, and bless you in your pilgrimage to eternity.

Your loving children, now and always."

ABOUT THE BOOK

What masterpiece nonfiction novel could listeners and readers of books hear at the youngest age possible, infancy (if book was being read to this age group) and thereafter, that would teach them the difference between respectable, moral, ethical, and Godly communications, behavior, and actions versus sinister, evil, and ungodly communications, behavior, and actions toward a child's or adult's siblings, friends, neighbors, community members, or during interactions with any other human they encounter in any society, religion, culture, city, country, or continent on this planet?

The answer is simple, succinct, and concise.

Two Sisters, The Dynamic Duo,
Pilgrimage To Eternity
Rachel Esther Lewis

Of course anyone reading this nonfiction novel to an infant or young child, acting in a mentor role, to teach that child the difference between honorable and Godly intentions, aspirations, perspectives, behavior, goals, endeavors, the correct definition of success, actions, and accomplishments would have translate the actual text in this spellbinding and instructive, life-guiding, and life-enhancing story written by its masterful author to the age-group being instructed and enlightened by its priceless content and mesmerizing, at times disappointing at first glance, then glorious destination and conclusions elucidated by this author in every word, paragraph, page, chapter, and most subtle and intriguingly, "between the lines" of this quintessential masterpiece of enlightenment and Godly teachings for the betterment of this world and all the citizens of every age, race, color, religion, culture, society, city, country, and continent.

It is near-impossible, though exceedingly rare and misguided readers might endeavor to pursue this unachievable task or ungodly goal, to argue that this story will not forever change the perspectives, aspirations, and intent of those enlightened by its content. Front cover to back cover, the reader will almost certainly immediately be uncontrollably attracted to, mesmerized by, and motivated to emulate the angelic two sisters and "shy away from" or "run most powerfully and at full-speed from" the despicable, sinister, and ungodly attitudes, behavior, and actions taken by the "bad actor" real-life characters and the undesirable, ill-advised pathway and journey through life that these "bad actors" pursued only to their own detriment and miserable death filled with guilt due to their "impossible to forget" evil treatment of these two sisters. In stark contrast, these two sisters that were maliciously targeted and disrespected, completely unwarranted and unjustified (in every respect), by these "bad actors," and who were the subjects of these sinister attackers' malevolent misconduct, were expectedly disappointed and, in a transient glance "devastated' by their siblings' or spouses' "less-than-admirable" behavior and actions, both sisters were nevertheless fully aware of their Godly intentions and aspirations to be messengers of God's Word, the Bible, and mentors to others whether their mentees honored and respected their teachings and enlightenment (which they delivered directly from God) to these individuals, or not.

The character traits made both these sisters indestructible "Superhumans," angelic mentors, and what most humans might reference and refer to as "Superheroes."

The irrefutable and eternal evidence of the unmatched angelic, powerful faith, and Godly lifelong actions and behavior of these two sisters, both of whom were quite similar to Joan of Arc, is the impression and impact these two sisters left on, or more concisely, bestowed upon every individual they met and interacted with on this planet.

The author witnessed first-hand the entire life pattern of behavior of "Two Sisters, The Dynamic Duo, Pilgrimage To Eternity" and awards this documentary film with one hundred percent of every academy award in every category, and in every aspect of their lives! If further proof of their story was requested, the author can also verify that not a single individual, never in the two sisters lives (except for the sinister "bad actors" exposed and revealed in this mesmerizing true story), ever were able to generate an honest word or description of discontent with the lives of both these angelic sisters, for they engaged in no immoral nor ungodly behavior their entire lives and did nothing but raise their children with the most caring, loving, God-respecting principles, teachings, prayers, and angelic kindness, wisdom, and enlightenment that any child could ever expect, and certainly not ever be disappointed by, but rather be eternally grateful for these God-empowered, God-sent, and God-redeemed and resurrected angelic "Two Sisters, The Dynamic Duo, Pilgrimage To Eternity," who were transiently gifted to this earth the first half of their pilgrimage and are now in the second and most-glorious half of their pilgrimage, which will continue for eternity!

ABOUT THE AUTHOR

The author supported, loved, and cherished these two angelic women, mothers, and mentors throughout her own life and these two sisters' extraordinary and immensely inspiring lives.

These real-life "Two Sisters, The Dynamic Duo, Pilgrimage To Eternity," in the author's insightful opinion, was, if filmed during their actual lives in real-time by the most famous and accomplished movie director and producer, would have recorded the most academy award nominations and awards won than any other story on this earth ever directed, produced, and preserved, for this generation and future generations, on film!

This masterpiece, intriguing, captivating, mesmerizing as written and as the nonfiction novel it is, serves as a guiding light, message for this generation, and warning for future generations with respect to consequences that may arise if siblings unjustifiably neglect, ignore, or abandon their love, kindness, and loyalty to their siblings or friends in life, or, in the even worse case scenario, take advantage of, manipulate, abuse, embarrass, disgrace, embezzle, or commit other sinful, evil, treacherous, and devastating actions that adversely impact their siblings, relatives, or other acquaintances and community members in their lifetime.

The author directly witnessed the zenith and glorious positivity, Godliness, humility, grace, mercy, kindness, ethical and moral behavior in all situations and always by these two sisters. Despite whatever evil and sinister attitudes, behavior, and actions by others that they encountered during their lives and interactions with all the humans they (met, were kind to, loved, encourage to be better humans, and respected nearly 99.9% of the time) interacted with during their shared journey, the magnitude and overwhelming positivity of their life perspectives, attitudes, intent, and actions always, in every case, massively outweighed, out-performed, and gloriously defeated the negativity that others attempted to instill or infect them with, in essence, attempting to decompress the Godly vacuum in every human soul, which, in these two sisters, had been filled to the brim, with one-hundred percent Godliness. These two sisters' souls (or "soul vacuums without God" in those who never seek or pursue God's guidance, grace, forgiveness of their sins, and mercy) were infinitely pressurized by God starting at their birth and throughout their childhood and adulthood and were impenetrable their entire lives!

Their existence and eternal legacy could not and will not be unrecognized or neglected by this author, nor should it be hidden or "brushed under the rug," but rather, like of beacon of light from Heaven, these angelic sisters will be given the "spot light in Hollywood as the A-list actors they were in this life," the only difference being that these two sisters never engaged in one second of "acting," but rather endeavored to and successfully accomplished infinity minutes of Godly mentoring of other humans from their birth, uninterrupted, to their spiritual eternal destination in Heaven with God!

Their astonishing, world-enhancing, and loving, kind lives must be always communicated to every generation and century, and recognized and attributed to their Godly behavior and guidance which they both accepted at birth and via the guidance given to them by their Godly parents, which they adhered to from birth until their "physical body death on earth" and glorious resurrection and commencement of their eternal life with their creator, guidance source and unparalleled mentor and provider of safety, strength, kindness, and love throughout their lives, God!

In summary, it is rare that an author, and readers worldwide of this revelatory, insightful, and enlightening masterpiece and bestseller, might (in the author's case, definitely will…) look forward to and dream of the day of his "physical body death on earth," which will then hasten his embarkment on and commencement of his next highly desired and anticipated reunion with these "Two Sisters, The Dynamic Duo, Pilgrimage To Eternity" angelic real-life blessings to this world, who positively guided, mentored, and led to the enormous unparalleled success, contentment, self-esteem, confidence, trust and faith in God, that shaped the life of the author and transformed the author into a fearless protector, defender, and messenger proclaiming and espousing worldwide humans and human rights, freedoms, respect, dignity, godly intent, aspirations, motivation, inspiration, goals, actions, success, and zenith accomplishments that can and only be fully recognized and achieved with the most astonishing, omniscient, omnipresent, and omnipotent and benevolent mentor of all generations and all centuries, God.